So she wanted him to pay attention to her, did she?

His silver eyes narrowed dangerously. Her soft rosy lips were pursed in that maddeningly desirable pout as she said his name. Kissing-shaped! That particular gesture had haunted him since first he beheld those red lips framing his name. It was too much for a soldier to endure. Bending toward the little witch, he pressed his own lips hard against that tantalizing softness. And pressed. And pressed . . .

His senses reeled. Instead of falling back or protesting or trying to remove herself, the little female actually caught at his shoulders to steady herself against the pressure of his mouth. She liked it!

The major raised his head, breathing with some difficulty. He discerned the girl was suffering from the same trouble. However, she recovered her breath more quickly than he did. Her voice reached him softly.

''That was . . . wonderful. Will you . . . do it again, please?''

THE RUNAWAY DEBUTANTE

Elizabeth Chater

FAWCETT CREST • NEW YORK

A Fawcett Crest Book
Published by Ballantine Books
Copyright © 1985 by Elizabeth Chater

Library of Congress Catalog Card Number: 85-90738

ISBN 0-449-20747-1

Manufactured in the United States of America

First Edition: December 1985

To
Richard Curtis

Prologue: Portman Square

London 1815

"You are telling me you have lost your entire fortune?" Lady Mountavon glared in horrified disbelief at her granite-faced spouse.

"To Tark," he confirmed. "But there's a way around the disaster."

Lady Amelia exhaled, shock and disapproval vying with a faint hope aroused by his last remark. His announcement had staggered even her iron self-control. "You are not telling me that the Earl of Tark is willing to forgive you your gambling losses?"

"For a suitable consideration, yes, he is."

"Consideration?" challenged his wife bitterly. "What else is left, if indeed you've lost it all to him already? A pint of your blood? Or mine?"

"Matilda." Lord Mountavon's voice was emotionless.

His wife's face whitened under her maquillage. "But how can she—"

"He is willing to marry her," said Lord George.

His wife was guilty of an openmouthed gape. Finally she stuttered, "*M-m-marry?* But he's the most notorious rake-hell in London! He's been denied a voucher to Almacks! Even

Hortensia Bullach, who has five ugly daughters to fire off, would not let that lecher within arm's length of them!''

''He wouldn't wish to be,'' snapped her exasperated husband. He was willing, in the cold light of the day after, to admit that he had acted the fool again in wagering beyond his means, but the fact that he had been able to make a recovery—or would be able to do so if his cold, straitlaced wife could be brought to see the advantages of the situation—had already done much to mitigate his self-reproach.

He began now, in a tone he considered to be calmly reasonable, to explain the compromise the earl had suggested. ''As you may be aware, Tark is in his fifties—''

''At least!'' interjected Amelia aggressively.

''—and he is desirous of having an heir,'' continued her husband as though she had not interrupted.

''Although England and possibly the Continent are peppered with his by-blows,'' his wife continued to comment nastily.

Her beleaguered spouse lost his temper. ''Will you hear me out? I should think you would be more than willing to learn how easily we may retain at least part of our fortune!''

''Fortune?'' sniffed the incorrigible Amelia. Then she relented. ''Yes, George, I am more than willing to learn how this miracle may be accomplished. But I must warn you that I would not trust the Earl of Tark if he came sponsored by an archbishop.''

''That is exactly what he wishes to do,'' her husband told her. ''He would marry a young, fresh biddable female of flawless lineage, and get some heirs upon her with all speed. I told him he might recover face in the ton if he wed a girl upon whom no breath of scandal has ever blown. And wed her with all pomp and circumstance.''

''He accepted that?'' mocked his wife, but already her shock and anger were dissipating into a kind of smug complacency. An earl was not so bad—even that one!

In his turn, her husband's expression became self-satisfied. "He said he'd never met the chit, but he did know something of our background—*'Never play against a stranger'* is his rule—so he agreed she would be ideal as a wife and mother. In fact, he wants to have the business over as soon as possible. He's going to visit friends in Italy for three weeks, which gives us time to have the banns called. The ceremony can take place as soon as he returns. He's paying the whole shot, of course."

"Of course," agreed his wife absently. She was already planning how best to manage the thing so as to wring as much consequence for herself as possible from it. "It is a pity your daughter is not a beauty, George." She preened herself. She had been a veritable diamond; some faint traces of her former beauty still remained.

With sensible caution, Lord George forbore to point out that those days were long past. Instead, pleased to have gotten over so much rough ground so lightly, he gave the flattering smile she expected.

"When will you tell the girl she's betrothed?" he asked.

"Oh, tomorrow will do," shrugged his wife. "She's such a mousy little creature that I'll have no trouble with her. I'll stress the fact that it's not every day a green miss is chosen by a member of the aristocracy."

"Let's hope she hasn't heard any of the stories about this particular aristocrat," grinned Mountavon. "She might cut up awkward."

"I shall handle it," promised Lady Amelia so grimly that for one vagrant moment Lord George felt a twinge of discomfort at the thought of the lamb being led to that particular sacrifice. He hardly knew the girl—Lady Amelia did not believe in saccharine, clinging family relationships and had relegated the child to nurses and a governess since the day of her birth—but he wondered how such a fledgling could deal with the vicious sophisticate he was giving her to. He

3

shrugged. Any alternative to Tark's plan involved disaster so horrendous that it would forever ruin any chance Matilda might have, as well as those of her parents.

As it happened, Miss Alford, Matilda's governess, had indeed heard of the Earl of Tark. When she beheld the white face and wide fear-darkened eyes of her beloved pupil, she immediately demanded to be told what had happened at the interview with her mama, in itself a very unusual occurrence. As Matilda told her, in a soft, shaken voice, Miss Alford's expression became more and more grim.

"You say this is already settled, my dear?" she asked when the tale was finished.

Matilda tried to smile. "Mama tells me I am the most fortunate female in nature," she quoted. "I—I had not heard of the Earl of Tark. But then, I haven't heard of many men, have I—not being allowed to go into society, nor to have any girl friends to chat with?"

Miss Alford set her teeth against the kind of diatribe she would have enjoyed launching against two of the most insensitive parents it had ever been her misfortune to encounter. Parents! They hardly ever saw the child; never arranged to do anything with her, even on her birthday or other holidays normally set aside for family sharing. Lord and Lady Mountavon were as cold and selfish a pair of human beings as Miss Alford had ever met. She was only thankful that they had employed her to take care of their lonely child and teach her the graces of social behavior.

The girl's mind was quick and bright. She had easily picked up not only the socially acceptable accomplishments, but also a good measure of solid education in more useful fields. Her governess had carried out this program to give Matilda a life raft. She had had a secret fear, a foreboding, that her darling charge might someday find herself compelled to make her own way in the world. Lord Mountavon's gambling was notorious. It had been only a matter of time until some catastrophe such as this present one occurred. Miss Alford had not envisioned anything as bad as the Earl of Tark, however. Even an obscure governess had heard of his licentious behavior. What were the Mountavons thinking of, to consider linking their only child to such a creature?

Miss Alford smiled bitterly. They were thinking of themselves, of course—of their comfort, their consequence, their pleasure—as they had always done. The governess set her jaw.

"We must appeal to your mama, Matilda. The earl is really not the man for you, my dear." As she spoke the words, she knew it was well-nigh hopeless. Still, she tried.

And was summarily dismissed from service for her pains. As was Matilda's personal maid, Polly.

"My daughter will not need you after she is married to Tark," Lady Amelia said coldly. "As for the girl who dresses my daughter, she will not do at all in the new world Lady Matilda is entering. I shall have to look for a smart dresser this week. Or perhaps I'll let Minip work with her. She has plenty of idle time as it is." Minip was Milady's dresser, a toplofty creature.

Miss Alford knew a moment's satisfaction at the situation that would occur when Lady Amelia realized just how much work the governess had been doing these last few years. "I hope she will be able to handle your correspondence and shopping," she murmured, but Lady Amelia was not listening.

The double loss, of Alford and Polly, devastated Matilda. She crept into Miss Alford's tiny room that night and demanded to be told the truth of the situation. "For, from what you have said, I gather that the earl of Tark is not a good man."

Miss Alford suspended her packing and sat down, drawing the girl to a seat beside her on the bed. "He has a very bad reputation," she began cautiously.

"In what way?"

What can I say? thought the governess in despair. Can I tell this innocent that he is a cruel, lecherous man? She will not understand what I mean! She has no notion of depravity!

"Are you afraid he will hurt me? Beat me?" prodded Matilda.

Miss Alford gathered her poise. "I am afraid he will abuse you in—in the marriage bed, a place where tenderness and gentle love should reign supreme." I am a fool, she thought, a romantic fool. Gentleness, in this house?

Matilda stared at her. "What shall I do?" she asked. Miss Alford had always had a maxim to fit any situation.

The governess put her hands against her head. "I do not know, my dearest child! If I could take you with me—! But I cannot! Your parents would only drag you back. Neither of us could stand against them." She put her arms around the girl. "I have failed you. All I can do is warn you. 'Forewarned is forearmed' . . . " she faltered.

Matilda raised her head from the governess's shoulder. Wiping her eyes, she said firmly, "I shall think of something." With a watery smile and a final hard hug, she slipped quietly from Miss Alford's room.

Chapter One

It was a very nasty night in London. Cold rain, whipped by a bitter wind, lashed down upon the dirty cobblestones. At the Cock and Pheasant Posting House (Proprietor, Matt Dodd), even the usual pandemonium of shouting grooms, grinding coach wheels, neighing horses, and infuriated passengers was muted into a dull rumble of discomfort.

Standing just under the meager shelter of the side entrance, two young women huddled wretchedly.

"It ain't yer fault we ain't got enough cash to buy us tickets out o' Lunnon," gasped the smaller of the two girls. "We'll just have to get me a job, like I said, and when I've saved enough—"

"Polly, we shall both find work," announced Lady Matilda Mountavon decisively. "It is absurd for us to be standing upon dignity when we are half-frozen and completely starved! Now come inside the inn with me, and we'll have a meal to put heart in us. And then we'll hazard our luck with the innkeeper. Surely so busy a hostelry must need two more excellent serving maids!"

Smiling, she ignored the other girl's muffled and not very convincing protests and led the way through the side door into the warm, well-lighted common room. Polly followed meekly. After a trying wait, they were at length able to secure seats at a large table crowded with grim-faced travelers. A harassed serving wench finally began to slop platefuls of food haphazardly in front of the muttering patrons, ignoring their complaints. Matilda, too hungry to talk, tasted the nondescript offering. Then she glanced around the greasy board for salt and pepper.

A woman seated across from her expressed Matilda's own opinion. "No taste to this grub," she sniffed.

Her sullen spouse snapped, "Well, it's 'ot," as though that were mercy enough in itself.

"We 'eard that their cook went an' lef' them without a word of warnin' today," gossiped a man next to Matilda. "It's a wonder they got even this much on the table." He chewed morosely. "Whatever it is."

Matilda's pale face began to brighten. Her eyes, a strange dark amber in color, seemed to give off golden light. Polly, glancing at her mistress, read the signs with a sense of alarm. Whenever Miss Matilda got one of her ideas, she looked just like a kitten about to pounce. She'd looked that way last night, when, comforting Polly after her brusque dismissal from Milord's service, Matilda had shared her plan to run away from a proposed marriage that revolted her every feeling.

"We'll slip away together before anyone's awake tomorrow," she proposed. "I know why Mama dismissed you, Polly. It wasn't because of anything you'd done or failed to do. It's because Papa has been gaming again and lost our whole fortune to the Earl of Tark."

Polly had gasped with dismay at this monumental disaster. It was notorious that one nobleman had lost a whole town and outlying farms, his family's total holding, in a desperate day and night at the gaming tables. His final act, which had been to put a period to his own life, did not seem to the little maidservant a very sensible solution to his problem. She wondered if the cold and cynical Lord Mountavon would proceed to such lengths and decided that he would not, as long as he had a young daughter of biddable disposition and impeccable lineage to use as barter. The servants' quarters had buzzed with tales of the licentious peer who was the winner of Lord Mountavon's fortune. The Earl of Tark's reputation was so deeply stained that he was avoided even by matrons with several daughters to launch. Surely, protested the servants, Lady Mountavon would not sell her only child to that vicious creature?

It seemed that Matilda's parents had exactly that stratagem in mind. When the news flew like wildfire through the mansion on Portman Square, Polly made no further objection to the plan of escape. But when they reached the posting inn, on foot and by devious back streets in the dawn, the fugitives discovered that Matilda's meager allowance, so carefully hoarded, was not enough to get them to another city where they might seek employment safely.

A whole day of searching for work brought only failure, since Matilda's skills—pianoforte, painting, and embroidery—while eminently suitable for a young woman of breeding, were not salable at hostels or coaching houses. Polly refused to leave her mistress, so neither one had been able to secure employment.

Now it was apparent to Polly that her mistress had had an idea that pleased her. Matilda stood up and moved purposefully off through the crowd of impatient travelers standing behind the chairs of more fortunate diners. Hastily wiping her crust of bread to catch the last few drops of gravy, Polly jumped up to follow her young mistress. It seemed that Lady Matilda had the inn kitchen as her destination. It was not hard to find it. She had only to follow the path of the hard-pressed serving maids.

The big room was in an uproar. In front of the two great stoves stood a large, stout woman wearing a mobcap slightly askew upon her graying hair. From the loud stream of commands, criticism, and appeals to heaven for help that she was issuing, the formidable dame was easily to be recognized as the wife of the owner of the inn.

" 'Tis plain why the Frenchies are forever raisin' riot and revolution!'' she was saying. "There's that Onree of ours, that my 'usband paid a king's ransom every month, walkin' out on us with nothin' in the oven for dinner! Unreliable— that's the Frenchies! If ever I take on another of 'em, may the good Lord forgive me, for I won't forgive myself!'' She glared around at her nervous staff. "An' per'aps someone will tell me where's the cook that promised to take Onree's place?''

With Polly hovering apprehensively at her shoulder, Matilda had been taking in the scene of confusion. She had never been in a public kitchen, but this one seemed reasonably well supplied with the necessary utensils. Perhaps they were not as clean as the ones Pierre had used in the Mountavon kitchen, but Matilda found herself very much at home with the whole situation. Obviously the treacherous Henri had had a good knowledge of his craft, for Matilda recognized jars and little tubs of exotic spices and herbs, now pushed out of the way by the amateur cooks.

Matilda seized the moment.

"I—" she began, then had to clear her throat. "*I* am the replacement for Chef Henri, ma'am.''

Her clear, young voice had managed to penetrate the din in the big room. Mrs. Dodd's eyes swiveled to her and took in, with one shrewd glance, the slight figure, plain dark cape, and pale yet determined face of the tall, slender woman who had just made the announcement. Mrs. Dodd frowned suspiciously and went at once on the attack.

"And where have you been, then, miss, while we've been tryin' to feed 'alf o' Lunnon? You're too late to do us any good . . . ''

All present knew this was merely a preliminary skirmish. Matilda smiled without replying as she stepped forward and

10

began lifting lids from the massive pots bubbling on the stoves.

"Garlic!" she demanded, waving a hand at one of the older kitchen wenches. "And that jar of laurel leaves. This chicken could be anything—or nothing!"

As the woman hastened to place the required items in Matilda's hands, Mrs. Dodd closed in on the interloper.

"And how would *your ladyship* know what it tastes like," she said with heavy mockery, "not having put so much as a morsel into your mouth?" She snorted rudely. "Onree was forever sippin' an' nibblin'."

"I have just finished eating the dinner you are serving in the common room," explained Matilda, still stirring as she added the seasonings she had requested. Then, maddeningly deliberate, she raised a ladleful of liquid to her lips, tasted, closed her eyes, nodded once, and stirred again.

Polly fought to contain her nervous giggles. Her mistress had just given an accurate imitation of Chef Pierre at his most Gallic. The performance was apparently impressive enough to soothe some of the anger and suspicion from Mrs. Dodd's face. She came closer.

"Aren't you goin' to take off your cloak?" she demanded.

Idly, as though the question had no great relevance to an artist at work, Matilda nodded again and lifted a spoonful of the liquid for Mrs. Dodd's approval. Gingerly, with due respect for the temperature of the broth, the host's wife tasted. Then a grudging yet relieved smile twitched at her lips.

"It'll 'ave to do, I suppose," she said, savoring the rest of the large spoonful. "Take yer cape off. An' 'oo is this?" indicating a grinning Polly.

"She is my helper. We both work for the one price," Matilda hastened to add, as Mrs. Dodd began to frown horrendously.

After a minute's sharp scrutiny, the innkeeper's wife nodded. She was not about to refuse the services of another kitchen helper, if they came free. "Better tell me your names, then. When dinner's over, I'll have Peg show you your room." She accepted their capes and handed them to the older serving woman.

"My helper is Polly," said Matilda quietly. "And I am called Merielle."

Now you've gone an' done it, miss! thought Polly in despair. Didn' you hear what she just said about Frenchies?

It appeared, however, that the French, while heartily disliked for many reasons—political, patriotic, and personal—were still regarded with a kind of awe for their culinary skills. With only a sniff to mark her opinion of all foreigners, Mrs. Dodd said firmly, "I shall call you Mary" and swept out of the kitchen.

The next few hours were too frantically crowded to permit of anything but complete attention to the cooking and serving of food. The maids, eager for their own sakes to placate their mistress, did all they could to help the new cook. Gradually a savory order emerged from the chaos. It was hard, challenging work for Matilda, but the skills required were not unknown to the girl. She had spent many clandestine hours in the homely comfort of the kitchen at Portman Square. It was the warmest room in that chill mansion, and the friendliest. During the innumerable hours when her governess, Miss Alford, had been required to attend Lady Mountavon as secretary or courier, the child had drifted into the cozy bustle downstairs, standing shyly near the door until invited by Chef Pierre, *"Entrez, petite mademoiselle!"* The chef had taken pity on the plain, forlorn little female and had gradually allowed her to observe his work and, eventually, to share his more arcane culinary secrets. Matilda had proved an apt and delighted pupil.

Miss Alford, inevitably learning of her pupil's extracurricular activities, had had only praise, and gratitude that the young girl was able to enjoy a little human warmth in her parents' gloomy, loveless mansion.

"A knowledge of haute cuisine will stand you in good stead when you have an establishment of your own, my dear," she had informed Matilda. "Just imagine how it will help you when some arrogant chef presents his proposed menus, all written in the French language and full of culinary terms!" And had improved the moment by insisting upon a renewed study of the language mentioned.

Matilda wisely decided, on this her first day at the Cock and Pheasant, not to attempt anything exotic. Quickly she identified the contents of the various stew pots. Beef in the largest. Potatoes and cabbage boiling together in one kettle, submerged to drowning in hot water. Turnips in another. Matilda ground fresh black pepper and garlic generously into the beef. She ladled the extra water from the now-soggy potatoes into a large soup kettle and placed the cabbage in a flat pan. Then she threw in great dollops of butter and a scoop of sugar with more pepper into the potatoes. She set Polly to mashing this mixture—one of her own favorites, although scorned by Pierre—while she herself put ham fat on a griddle to render and brown. Soon she was able to set out plates of well-seasoned beef slices, cabbage with a drench of savory ham fat, turnips lightly dusted with cinnamon, and the mouth-watering mashed potatoes. The maids, invited to taste, rolled ecstatic eyes and licked hungry lips.

Very shortly the serving maids were returning with empty plates and requests for second helpings from the diners in the Commons. This necessitated a fresh burst of activity as vegetables were peeled and put into the already-boiling vegetable water Matilda had poured off to save for soup. While they worked, she instructed Polly and the kitchen wenches as Chef Pierre had instructed her.

"Never use too much water in preparing vegetables," she told them. "The taste goes into the water, and then you have

13

to throw it out. Of course you could make soup or gravies or a stew with it if you wished. I'll show you that later. But now we must get more food ready for Mrs. Dodd's guests." She peered into the nearest kettle. "Have we enough meat, do you think? I am not yet familiar with the requirements of your customers."

"There won't ever be enough if you plan to heap up the plates like you been doin'," came the sharp voice of the host's wife. "They think it's Christmas out there, what with second helpin's an' all! You must serve smaller portions, Mary," scolded her employer, but the other servants could tell that she was pleased at the new cook's success.

Mrs. Dodd's wary euphoria continued for several days. Matilda concealed her self-doubts and tremors successfully, and, aided by the admiring Polly, managed to revise the menus of the Cock and Pheasant so tastily that the word spread even among the residents of the area, who came to join the travelers at the board. Business in the Commons doubled. Of necessity, the amounts of money Mrs. Dodd was required to lay out upon provisions also increased, but her strictures and grumblings were remarkably mild as she totaled the profits at the end of each day. She was not one to fly in the face of manifest Providence and had soon decided not to challenge her very unusual new cook.

"She ain't no beauty," Mrs. Dodd told her spouse, "but she's got pretty eyes, kind of like a cat's. And she *can* cook."

Host Dodd privately considered that the new cook's best feature was her mouth. The beautifully cut lips, a soft rosy pink, reminded him of strawberries. Knowing his wife, he was wise enough to keep such romantic thoughts to himself and contented himself with admitting that the girl could cook.

"Sort of a foreign moniker she's got, ain't it? Maryell or whatever it is. Did she tell you what 'er last name is?"

"No, an' I didn' ask," snapped his wife. "If she's some

sort of foreigner—though that's hard to believe, considerin' the way she talks—you an' me don't want to get mixed up in her troubles.''

"She don't talk like no foreigner I ever heard," objected Dodd. "More like a poor relation or a 'anger-on of one of the nobs. Maybe you'd best sniff 'round a bit. We don't want to get mixed up in nothin' havey-cavey.''

"One o' the nobs in my kitchen?" sneered Mrs. Dodd. "That I cannot believe!"

However, watching Matilda carefully the following day, Mrs. Dodd had to admit the girl presented a problem. She was no kitchen wench. Her accent was better than any usually heard in the Commons, and the chit Polly treated her more like a mistress than a fellow servant. Mrs. Dodd decided to get to the bottom of the mystery. She chose her moment shrewdly.

"It's time you told me who you are an' where you come from,'' she opened abruptly late that evening, catching the weary girl on her way up to her room in the attic.

Matilda's shocked expression at once confirmed Mrs. Dodd's suspicions.

"Have I not satisfied your requirements as a cook?" faltered the girl, looking mighty guilty.

This weak challenge still gave the host's wife pause. Granted, such an answer was enough to make a looby think; it also reminded Mrs. Dodd that she had stumbled upon a rare article in Mary Whatever-her-name-was. In fact, a jewel, since Mary and Polly together worked for less than Mr. Dodd had had to pay the treacherous Onree. Did she really want to discover that her fine new cook should be somewhere else than in the kitchen of the Cock and Pheasant? If trouble did come, the Dodds could always say they'd been gulled by a smooth-tongued adventuress. Her curiosity fully aroused, Mrs. Dodd pressed for an answer.

Matilda recalled the teachings of Miss Alford. *Honesty is*

the best policy. Would it work in this situation? She was too tired to invent a convincing lie. Matilda shrugged fatalistically. "I am a runaway noblewoman. My father was forcing me to marry a very wicked earl—"

Any further disclosures were halted by the broad grin that spread across Mrs. Dodd's face. She shook her head in reluctant admiration. "If ever you lose your job with me, Mary, you could get another right away makin' up plays for one o' them theaters in Drury Lane. 'Runaway noblewoman,' you says! That's a ripe un! I'll warn Dodd not to let any wicked earls into the Commons, lest they steal you away from us."

She stumped away down the corridor, chuckling afresh at the fertile imagination of her wily cook.

Matilda was left to admire, yet again, Miss Alford's wisdom, and the advisability of always telling the truth.

Chapter Two

Although Polly still glanced anxiously around the Commons a dozen times a day, fearful that the Mountavons would suddenly burst through the door seeking their runaway child, Lady Matilda herself seemed to be quite calm and happy with their new estate.

"I should like to let dear Alford know we are safe and well," she said one morning while she and Polly were working with the kitchen maids in a thorough washing of the tables.

"Do ye know where she went to, milady?" asked Polly, and then caught herself at Matilda's warning glance. "I mean *miss*."

"Oh, yes, she told me where to find her if ever I should have need of her," answered Matilda somberly. "I think it worried her very much to have to abandon me to my fate."

"She'd have been glad you got away from that Tark," averred Polly stoutly. "I'm sure she knew we'd be all right."

Matilda smiled but decided to send a message to the address in Brighton that Miss Alford had given her. The governess had always been closer to her than either of her parents, and would be pleased to hear that her pupil had managed to find honest employment. She could claim that she had the full cooperation of the Dodd servants and the respect, at least, of her employers.

After nearly two weeks without a sign from her parents, Matilda was ready to believe that she had truly escaped the ugly destiny they had planned for her. She tried to feel regret at the thought of her father's destitute condition, but there had never been any sort of tenderness or even rapport between them. He had obviously been willing to use her cold-bloodededly in any way that would solve his difficulties, no matter how repulsive or degrading such use would be for her.

Squaring her shoulders, Matilda scanned the shining tables with satisfaction. "Very well done!" she praised the maids, and led them back to the kitchen for a restorative snack before the heavy work of the day began.

That evening an even larger crowd than usual thronged the Commons, clamoring to be fed. When the coach from Portsmouth pulled up in front of the inn, Mrs. Dodd came running in to rally her troops. Every maidservant in the house must join in serving the meal.

"That means you, Polly." She glared. "I've seen the way you 'ang about in 'ere as if you was afraid of the customers!"

With an anxious look at Matilda's reassuring expression, Polly ran off to the Commons with the other girls.

She was back in two minutes, her face white.

"Milady!" she whispered. "It's yer papa's groom! He's standin' in the doorway, peerin' about as if he was looking for someone!"

"Then, you must stay safely in here with me, to help me serve the plates and prepare more vegetables," said her mistress firmly. "Joby," she smiled sweetly at the kitchen boy, "Miss Polly will take care of your jobs now. Do go into the Commons and bring back the dirty plates and cups."

This exchange of duties pleasing both the persons concerned, Matilda was able to draw a deep breath and consider the full import of Polly's news. If indeed Lord Mountavon had become so desperate as to send his grooms into every posting house around London, then perhaps she and Polly were not as safe as she had imagined. Could the girl have been mistaken? Hardly, for Jake was a huge bully of a fellow, with a sullen, lowering countenance. A memorable face.

Must they leave London, then? Matilda frowned. While she could not go so far as to say she loved the hard, menial work, still she had enjoyed the sense of self-reliance, the freedom it gave her to know she was able to provide for her own needs and keep a roof over her head by her own efforts. She had even saved every penny of the wages Mrs. Dodd gave her. There might be enough for a trip to some other city, where Mountavon's servants could never find her. Brighton, to Miss Alford? But no! That was probably the first place they would search. Whether they had already done so or not, Matilda could not risk putting her dear governess in jeopardy. She frowned and might have fallen into a minor fit of the dismals if Mrs. Dodd had not chosen that moment to bustle into the kitchen, loudly complaining that Mary's new menu, giving the customers a choice, was far less efficient than her own former way of serving a set meal.

"But think how the profits have grown, ma'am!" reminded Matilda, finding it impossible to be disturbed by such a trifling matter when her father's groom might be prowling through the inn at this very moment. She shot a wary glance at the open doorway.

Of course, Mrs. Dodd caught it. She surveyed the kitchen suspiciously. "Why is Polly here with you, instead of serving, as I ordered?"

"Because we are used to each other's ways, and can save time at dishing out," said Chef Merielle with Gallic hauteur.

Mrs. Dodd was not bamboozled. Her suspicions sharpening into certainties, she said slowly, "Ye've both run away from somethin', haven't ye? And yer extra worried right now.

19

Is there a constable in the Commons? Is that why yer hidin' in here?''

Her expression told Matilda clearly that Mrs. Dodd thought she had them in her power now. *Escaping from authorities!* Would the host's wife turn them over summarily, or help them avoid the law? The narrow smile on Mrs. Dodd's fat face gave her the answer. Their employer would hide them, but at a price.

"I'll be talkin' to ye both later," she promised, and flounced out of the kitchen.

In the push of maids moving past the stoves to collect the well-laden plates, Matilda had no time to make any important decisions, but she promised herself she would find a way to leave the posting house the following day. She and Polly had nothing but her hoarded allowance and the two weeks wages they had already received. Still, it would make enough to pay coaching fares to some other town, where, with their newfound confidence, they might easily obtain employment at an inn.

An hour later Polly made a furtive reconnaissance and could find no trace of the burly Jake. She did, however, see something else that stirred her romantic young heart to its core. She came to Matilda with a used plate.

"Can you put some choice, tender bits on this one, miss?" she whispered. "The cuts you call fork-tender?"

Matilda smiled at the urgent expression on Polly's vulnerable little face. "Have you seen a handsome youth you'd like to cosset?" she teased.

Polly's eyes opened wider. "Oh, no, miss! It's a soldier in a fine uniform—with one sleeve pinned up. Such a sad look in his eyes, he has, but he's a fine figure of a man for all that!"

Much interested, Matilda prepared a well-done, toothsome plate of her best offerings and handed it to the girl. After Polly had thankfully departed, Matilda indulged her curiosity. She had never seen quite that look upon her little maid's face before. Who or what could have caused it? Without thinking too much about her motives, she slipped through the kitchen door into the Commons.

The large room was badly overcrowded, well-lighted, and full of a din, most of it cheerful. It wasn't hard to spot Polly's absurd mobcap, since as usual she had managed to get it askew on her curls. The big man she was bending over stood out, too, even in that crowd. In the orange glow of the candles, his weather-beaten countenance looked like one of the paintings Miss Alford had taken her to see at a museum. Dark; dark and strong; the face of a man who had met the worst life could fling at him, and conquered it. Matilda drew a wavering breath.

Black hair, cut short on a classic head. A strong nose, an even stronger mouth, just now relaxed into a grin of pleasure, but heavily marked with grooves that shouted self-control. Broad shoulders in the neat military coat—and, yes, one sleeve pinned up. So that is why Polly needed tender meat, she thought, with deep pity. It must be hard to cut with only one hand!

And then, almost as though aware of her scrutiny, the proud head lifted, and across that smoky, noisy room his hawk-gaze met hers. His eyes were almost colorless! Were they gray? Silver? The palest blue? Matilda's breath caught in an unconscious shock. Framed in black brows and heavy black lashes, the soldier's eyes were the most challenging— the most frightening—she had ever encountered. She started to slip back into the kitchen, away from that powerful confrontation.

At this moment, Polly's head rose and turned toward her. The soldier had evidently asked a question as to her identity. Polly smiled over toward her mistress and said a few quiet words. Then she came over toward Matilda, who promptly vanished into the kitchen. There Polly ran her to earth.

"Oh, milady, it's like the answer to prayer!" she began,

keeping her voice low with an obvious effort. "The soldier is in need of a cook—of a whole staff of servants!—an' he's going to leave for Scotland as soon as he can hire them!"

Matilda tried to take it in. A thousand objections, fears, doubts, thronged into her mind, chief of which was that the big man was playing a game on Polly, such teasing as it seemed men enjoyed when they talked with serving women. She tried to bring Polly to a less excited state.

"Who is this soldier? Why did he tell you he needed servants? Was he trying to hire you?"

Polly drew a deep, sobering breath. "It's all so wonderful, milady, just like one o' them stories Miss Alford used to tell us about heroes comin' to the rescue in the nick o' time—!"

"*Polly!*" urged her mistress firmly.

Polly began again. "He told me how much he an' his friend enjoyed their dinner. Quite the nob he is, milady! Talks just like your papa and his friends. Only more polite," she amended. "Well, I tells him my friend—" she ventured a wary glance at Matilda, which was greeted with a smile, "—Merielle had made it, and how you was the best cook in Lunnon. Then *he* says, 'Is she happy in this place?' an' gave it a pretty shrewd look. I says you was anxious to get away from Lunnon, and that's when he tells me he needs a cook and other servants. I thought of Fredricks right off," Polly ended wistfully.

Whatever Matilda might have been going to say remained unsaid as she considered this striking idea. Fredricks, who had been butler to the Mountavons since before her own birth, had been dismissed last year as summarily as Miss Alford two weeks ago. Lady Amelia had complained that he was too old and doddering to handle his duties, and had replaced him without ceremony. Miss Alford had kept in touch with the old man, and said he was living rather unhappily in a small village outside London. Would it be possible that she could

22

persuade this soldier to employ the older man? Fredricks was devoted, and knowledgeable, and loyal.

"What else did the soldier say?" she asked Polly.

"Why not let me tell you myself?" came a deep, husky voice at her shoulder.

Matilda whirled. It was the big man from the Commons, and behind him stood a gaunt figure in the dress of a sergeant.

"May I introduce myself?" the deep voice went on, but Matilda hardly heard it, so striking was the close-up impact of the huge officer before her. His face had been darkened by exposure to all sorts of weather, and lined with pain. Still, it was a good face, strong and handsome in a style wholly male. Even in the strange light eyes, there was no hint of weakness, no vulnerability revealed. It flashed across Matilda's mind to wonder if indeed this big man ever let himself go unshielded—which was a stupid idea, she challenged herself, in view of the wary presence of his sergeant at his shoulder. Yet the thought persisted, even in clear view of those pale, dark-fringed eyes.

The other three—Polly, the sergeant, and the big officer—all had their eyes on her face and were obviously waiting.

"Well?" demanded the officer.

To her horror, Matilda felt a deep blush burning her cheeks. "I'm sorry," she stammered. "I didn't hear what you said."

It was feeble. It was absurd. The big man's heavy eyebrows rose quizzically, and the faintest hint of a smile tugged at his lips. "Now, I wonder why that was?" he mused in a gentler voice. "You seemed to be paying attention—to something?"

Matilda straightened her shoulders. "I was wondering if you ever left yourself undefended?" she heard herself say, honestly.

The officer laughed ruefully. "It's not a habit calculated to prolong life, where I've been," he admitted. "Now, if I have your attention, ma'am?'' and he waited, the smile at his lips definitely mocking.

"You have," promised Matilda, setting her teeth against his derision.

"I am Major Robert Bruce of the Royal Highlanders, and this is my friend, Sergeant Ronal McLeod. We are hoping to hire a full complement of staff for my home in Scotland, and Miss Polly seemed to feel that you might be able to help us." He paused, but when she did not immediately reply, he continued quietly, "The matter is really urgent, ma'am. I must take possession of my—new home as quickly as possible."

"In Scotland, I understand?" ventured Matilda. "Would you not be wiser to hire staff from among the locals, thus causing less resentment against a newcomer?"

"Well thought of," remarked the big major with what Matilda decided was odious condescension. "Except for the fact that my—ah—predecessor managed to alienate the surrounding population so completely that I'm told by the lawyers I will be fortunate if I can buy provisions within two hundred miles of the castle."

This was exciting stuff indeed! A lonely Scottish castle, ringed round with sullen or angry natives, with the small garrison under constant, if covert, siege! Matilda's eyes began to sparkle like a hunting kitten's. The big soldier looked at her carefully, then a slow grin, quite unlike his former rather weary cynicism, softened his expression.

"That interests you, does it?" he murmured. "Ready for a challenge, are you, ma'am?"

Ready or not, Matilda got one at that moment. Mrs. Dodd swept into the kitchen at her most formidable.

"And what is goin' on here, if I may ask?" she hooted. "There's a dozen guests clamorin' for their dinner in the Commons, Mary, and you lollopin' about here with these soldiers! I'll have to have better'n that from you, if I'm to keep you on in my kitchen!" It was an open threat, Matilda

24

realized. Mrs. Dodd was ready to capitalize on the weakness she had noticed in her new cook.

It had suddenly become an intolerable situation. For whatever reason—the sudden appearance of Jake, the suspicion aroused in her employer, the resultant efforts of the latter to manipulate and control her—suddenly Matilda's position had become impossible to endure. It was past time to make the needed break to any place away from London. With the planned wedding scarcely a week off, efforts to find the runaway would be doubled, and would probably succeed. So the officer's proposal suddenly seemed a lifesaver.

"I'll go with you," she said quietly, giving the big man a searching scrutiny. "Polly, too."

"Of course," agreed her new employer. He regarded her soberly and then smiled at the quivering Polly. "Go to your rooms and pack," he said.

"They'll do no such thing!" interjected Mrs. Dodd furiously. "What's goin' on? Are you stealin' my servants, then?"

"Have you a contract, indentures?" asked the major quietly.

"No, but I know things about these two that they wouldn't want noised around Lunnon! Ain't that so, *Merielle*?" she jeered.

"We have nothing to get but our small handbags," began Matilda, ignoring the threat.

"I'll get 'em, an' our capes!" offered Polly eagerly.

"I'll go with you, to make sure you don't steal anything!" snapped Mrs. Dodd. She was obviously upset by the development but could not think of a way to stop its progress. The major gave a nod to his sergeant, who followed the departing females unobtrusively.

When they were gone, Matilda began to have second thoughts. "I can't just leave her in the middle of dinner!" she began.

"The crowds have thinned considerably," the major told her. "It won't hurt her to serve her guests for once." He glanced around the kitchen. "Did you really prepare the food that was served tonight?"

"Yes. But I am not really a cook," began the girl.

"You'll do me," smiled the major. "But then, after army grub and bub, almost anything would taste good."

Raising shocked and angry eyes to his face, Matilda was confronted with the most delightful, teasing grin she had ever beheld. A strange warmth began to burn in her breast, and she could hardly meet that pale, inquiring gaze. Finally she began to chuckle.

"As an inducement to become your cook and hire your servants for you, that last remark was hardly successful," she said in minatory tones.

Her opponent was not deceived. "You are just as anxious to leave this—establishment as I am to have you," he told her, with a firmness she began to find disturbing. Was the creature going to take over her life as well as her services in the kitchen?

He was continuing, "I don't know what hold that harpy has over you, but evidently it is not a powerful one, or she would be acting with female arrogance—"

"We must have one thing very clear," Matilda found herself saying. "There will be no displays of arrogance, either female or male, while we work for you, Major Bruce." As she scanned his face to observe the effect of this pronouncement, Matilda was surprised to see a sudden new intentness in his expression.

"Say it again!" her new employer commanded. "My name. Please."

"Major Bruce," the girl complied. "Have I got it wrong?" she faltered.

The irritating creature grinned. "No, that's correct. I shall expect to hear it often upon your lips."

Shaking her head in rising wonder that she might have hired herself to a loony, Matilda asked, "Where do we go now?"

The rather bemused expression was wiped from his features at once, to be replaced by a smile. "You are really willing to trust yourself and your friend to my care? It gives me a very good feeling to receive such unquestioning acceptance! As the new laird of a rather hostile clan, I'm going to need all the acceptance I can find."

Matilda was privately of the opinion that this big man with the strong face and the remarkable eyes would never lack for adherents—especially female ones. But such thoughts ill beseemed her, she decided, as his future cook. That thought brought others in its wake. Matilda resolved to act with stern decisiveness.

"How large a staff will you need, Major Bruce?" she began. "I have some excellent candidates in mind."

His gaze rested on her small flushed face in amusement. "Ever practical!" he said softly. "Obedient, too."

Matilda wondered what he was talking about now, but since Polly arrived at that moment, bearing their small bags and escorted by the silent sergeant, she did not ask for enlightenment. Instead she watched with pleased surprise the major's superb mastery of the logistics of a sticky situation. Within a few moments, he had silenced, if not pacified, the irate Mrs. Dodd, paid her husband generously for the meal he and his sergeant had eaten, added a startlingly generous tip, which Mrs. Dodd absentmindedly pocketed, and arranged for a hackney to take his party to the nearest hostel.

When the coach was on its way, Matilda caught her first deep breath in the last quarter of an hour. "Was it wise of you to let the Dodds know where we are to be found?" she ventured softly.

Major Bruce chuckled reprehensibly, and even the taciturn Sergeant McLeod barked a laugh.

"It would have been very poor tactics indeed, in view of

27

her threats, had I intended to stay in that particular inn," he admitted brazenly. "However, when we are sufficiently removed from her scrutiny, I intend hailing our jarvey and giving him different orders."

Relieved, but marveling at the devious nature of her new employer, Matilda lapsed into exhausted silence, clasping Polly's hand firmly as the coach rolled through the dark streets of London.

"There is still one mystery that we must clear," her new employer broke the silence suddenly. "Your name. Polly called you Miss Matilda; the host's wife called you Mary, and then Merielle. Would you like to tell me which it is? If any of them?"

An alarming suspicion had entered the major's mind. If her name really was Merielle, and with that well-bred voice and her little unconscious air of dignity, she might well be one of the unfortunate aristos escaped from turbulent France. He turned broad shoulders for a better look at her in the gloom of the carriage.

Although his voice had not been hostile, nor particularly mocking, Matilda felt indignation. *"If any of them,"* forsooth! What did he think she was? "I am Matilda—" she began haughtily, and then recollected herself just as Polly's hand squeezed warningly over hers. "—uh—Policy," she gulped.

The big soldier gave a sardonic laugh.

"As in: Silence is the best policy?" he taunted. "If I am to take you into my household in dangerous terrain, I must at least know your right name, and be aware of any potential danger you may represent to me."

Matilda considered this. He was correct, of course. Even she could see the folly of entering a strange and hostile arena without confidence in the supporters at one's back. Had she not had the faithful and loving Polly during these last difficult days . . . !

"My name is Matilda. I used the name Merielle when I applied for the position in the Dodds' kitchen because they had just lost a much-valued French chef, and I had been instructed in cuisine by one of the same." She was aware of light eyes gleaming at her, but there was no feeling of menace. Instead she felt a sort of acceptance of herself that she had seldom encountered. She explained slowly, "I have always disliked my name, possibly because Miss Alford told me it meant 'mighty battle-maid.' So inappropriate! I have never been—aggressive. I have always wished to bear a musical, feminine name like—like Merielle . . . " Her voice lingered on the syllables sweetly. "For special occasions only, of course," she hastened to add, fearing that the soldier would think her a romantic idiot.

"For special occasions, then," agreed the man. What was he getting himself into? Lumbering himself with a plain, small female of mysterious background, who was not even willing to admit to her own name? But something about her appealed to his quirkish sense of humor. He began to grin. "At all other times, *Matilda*. I believe I can use a mighty battle-maid in the conflict I am facing."

There was something in that deep male voice that sent a frisson along Matilda's skin. Miss Alford's maxims rushed through her memory, clamoring. *Look before you leap! A pinch of caution is worth a pound of regret . . . !*

The dark velvet voice interrupted her panicky musings.

"Ma—til—da?" it wheedled softly. "Is my mighty battle-maid having second thoughts?"

She could tell he was laughing at her, daring her to show courage. Very well! She squared her small shoulders.

"Matilda Mountavon at your service, Major Bruce."

The soldier's only answer was a chuckle.

Chapter Three

The following morning, after a superb breakfast in the large, well-patronized inn the major had finally selected, Matilda and Polly congratulated themselves upon their good fortune. It was not enough that they had shared a room of the first consequence, even elegance, with the added benison of enough cans of hot water to supply two hip-baths, and sheets as clean as any they had ever slept on. It was not enough that they had eaten breakfast in a private parlor, with the courteous company of two well–set-up soldiers to make it pleasant. No, in addition to these boons, they had been informed, over breakfast, of the whole problem that faced their new employer—and Matilda had discovered that she could indeed prove her worth by making practical and helpful suggestions. It was with a real sense of pleasure that Matilda was able to give Major Bruce the name and address of Fredricks, whom she assured him was not only knowledgeable as a butler, but up to any rig or row a disgruntled community might seek to employ against her new master. Then she asked if Major Bruce needed a housekeeper?

It struck the girl that Major Bruce might not be paying her his full attention, since his eyes appeared to be centered upon her mouth rather than on her own eyes, as one might expect in a business discussion.

"Major Bruce?" she reminded him.

The big soldier pulled himself back to the conversation with some reluctance. *"Oh, yes!"* he said, apropos of nothing she was aware of.

"I have the very lady to serve as housekeeper for you, if you need one," Matilda repeated. "Her name is Alford."

"She has been housekeeper where you worked?"

Mention of her governess reminded Matilda of the many maxims that the latter had loved to impart. *Honesty is the best policy,* she reminded herself, and a naughty smile curled her lips as she remembered how well that particular maxim had worked to protect her at the Dodds' inn. Still, she knew somehow that with this big soldier she had better act with complete honesty. He is, she told herself, in a difficult enough situation with all the countryside against him, without having traitors within his household! With this commendable purpose, she informed him briefly as to her reasons for leaving Portman Square and seeking work as Chef Merielle at the Cock and Pheasant.

When she had finished, Matilda was rather surprised to observe the stunned looks upon the faces of both the soldiers. "Exactly how old are you?" demanded the major.

"I am twenty-five," announced Matilda, crossing her fingers under the table.

Sergeant McLeod muttered something, and the major gave her a challenging glance.

"As we say in the army, *Pull the other one,*" the major snapped. "The truth, please. At once!"

What had made him so angry? wondered Matilda. "I am not sure it is any of your business, even if you are my employer," she began a little hotly.

"I could be jailed for contributing to the delinquency of a minor," Major Bruce told her coldly. "Your correct age, if you please."

Quelled, Matilda told him. Major Bruce breathed a sigh of

relief. "Although it is probably not the thing socially, you are at least old enough to be on your own," he admitted grudgingly. "But I must reconsider my offer—in all fairness to yourself, child."

"I am not a child," snapped Matilda. "I have found a job, earned my living—"

"For all of two weeks," interjected the major nastily.

"If you do not wish to hire me, I shall leave you at once and find a new position," threatened Matilda firmly. "Here."

Unexpectedly a new voice entered the argument. "What if Jake finds us here? He nearly caught us at Dodds'."

"Who is Jake?" The major frowned.

"One of my father's grooms."

The major sighed. "I knew it was too good to last," he announced cryptically. "I suppose I had better see you back to your parents this morning."

He was not quite prepared for the ashen faces that confronted him. Surely it would not be so bad? The lovely girl would be punished, of course, but no parent could remain angry long at such a little charmer! He summoned up a smile. "They may screech a bit, but they'll be so glad to get you safe home . . . " he offered.

"They will make her marry that monster, and he will hurt her and make her sick as he does all his women!" flared Polly. "The upper servants have been talking about him. I won't let you force her back!"

"Just who is this *monster* you are so fearful of?" demanded the major.

"It is the Earl of Tark," said Matilda in a dead-sounding voice. "I suppose you have not heard of him—"

But a remarkable change had come over the major's face. "*Tark?* You tell me your parents are willing to give you to that man? I cannot believe—"

"My father lost everything to him over the gaming ta-

32

bles," said Matilda, picking up a thread of hope at his re-
vulsive attitude. "It seems the earl wants legitimate sons to
inherit his titles, and my birth and breeding are good enough
to satisfy him, since it appears he has little choice among the
suitable females in the haut ton."

Major Bruce was glaring at Sergeant McLeod, who shook
his head reluctantly. "We can't let little miss go back to *that
lecher*, sir," he muttered.

The big man groaned. "Then, we'd best get her out of
England and safe in Scotland before—uh—Jake or one of the
other grooms finds her," he said reluctantly. He turned a not
very approving eye upon the two females. "You'd better keep
to your room until I can get the arrangements made for our
departure. What was the butler's address, again? And the
housekeeper's? Perhaps between them, they can hire a few
other servants and meet us at the border. McLeod, I'll send
you to them with money for the trip north."

This arrangement did not suit the sergeant, who was obviously unwilling to leave his master at this crucial time, but
Major Bruce insisted and had him off within the hour, with
elaborate directions as to the meeting place.

With a final reproachful glance at the women, the sergeant
left. Bruce then turned his attention to Matilda and her maid.
"I thought I told you to go to your room?" he said coldly.

"I had to know what your plans were," protested Matilda.
"How else could I protect you?"

This remark seemed to amuse the big soldier. "Is that what
you're doing?" he queried. "I somehow got the impression
it was the other way around."

This reply, for some reason, restored the warm glow that
Matilda had noticed in the region of her chest.

"You have been more than kind," she offered, a little
shyly, remembering her manners. "Our lovely room, every
attention to our comfort—! We are deeply grateful, Major
Bruce!"

This remark seemed to restore the major's good humor. "I hope it may prove so, at the right moment," he said obscurely. "In the meantime, will you *please* retire to your room until I have made all the arrangements for our trip to Scotland? Unless, of course, you wish to come and choose my new carriages, horses, and the like?"

"Oh, are you planning on making such extensive purchases, Major Bruce? Are you sure you have enough money? Prices have risen alarmingly during the war, sir," she suggested.

The major rose, grinning, and pulled her to her feet. "Go, Madame Chef!" he commanded. "Before I do what I've been aching to do since first I heard you pronounce my name!"

For some unknown reason, Matilda found this jocular threat enough to put her all about, and she almost scuttled as she left the private parlor, with Polly in close attendance, and sought the privacy and safety of the bedroom. Polly, for once, was no help, going on about the major's good looks, and his charm, and such other irrelevancies, until Matilda could have screamed. Finally the maid ceased her panegyrics and turned a quizzical eye upon her mistress.

"And don't tell me you don't think 'e's a stunner, milady, because I won't believe you." She grinned as widely as the major.

Matilda did not have the heart to deny the girl's absurd comment. Polly had been most loyal and helpful, and it would be poor repayment to tell her she was, in this instance, completely mistaken in her evaluation of her mistress's feelings.

Chapter Four

As they entered Major Bruce's new carriage the following morning, it was evident to both girls that money had been no object in the purchase. It was, in point of fact, the grandest, most impressive, most comfortable equipage either girl had ever ridden in, as its remarkably smooth progress over the cobblestones of the city streets proved.

And six horses! Mettlesome beasts they were, Polly cried admiringly, peering out one window at an impossible angle. Two outriders on horseback, she marveled, and at least one wagon filled with boxes and trunks, following smartly behind!

"It's like a king's progress!" breathed the little maid, pulling herself in and staring with wide-eyed admiration at the major.

"I'm glad you like it," said the soldier, with a small smile. He turned toward Matilda, seated on his other side, and discovered that she, too, was leaning forward and trying to peer back along the street. He touched her shoulder. "Are you impressed, too?" he asked, and there was no disguising the amusement in his expression.

Matilda beamed back at him. "You must be richer than Croesus," she sighed.

Major Bruce laughed aloud. "Hardly! Wasn't he the one who turned everything he touched into gold?"

"No, I think that one was Midas." Matilda frowned in an effort to recall Miss Alford's teaching. "At any rate, I don't think I wish to compare you to either of them, since as I remember now, they both had an unhappy time." She sighed with pleasure, settling back into the padded squabs of the carriage with a luxurious wiggle that brought a grin to the man's lips.

"You are saying you wish me to have smooth sailing?" he inquired.

The huge golden eyes, now shimmering with contentment, focused on his bold, dark soldier's face. "Yes, I do. In fact, if it were not unforgivably rude, I would wish that you would tell me the whole story of your inheritance, and especially why you must rush north to Scotland with a full staff of servants. Do none of the old retainers remain loyal to the name? Why do they hate their new laird?"

"It is not so dire as that," began the major, settling himself comfortably against the squabs as Matilda had done and patting the neatly folded sleeve of his jacket into place. "It seems, from what my men-at-law tell me, that my predecessor, who was a great-uncle on my father's side, was a crusty old miser, a true curmudgeon who pinched every groat until it screamed and refused to spend a bawbee in repairing any of the tenants' huts or farm buildings. He always managed to hold off paying for any service until the poor tradesman had almost forgotten the debt, but he insisted that payment for any bill *he* presented be made on demand. A most unpleasant landlord, in fact. It is no wonder to me that everyone in the vicinity hated him."

Matilda nodded agreement. "He does seem a thoroughly unpleasant character," she admitted. "But you are not he! Why should they all hate you?"

"I," announced the major in a theatrical voice, "am even worse! A Sassenach, no less, and who is to say—"

But the girl, chuckling, had interrupted him. "What is this Shassenash? I hope it is not a bad word?"

"In many parts of Scotland, that is exactly what it is," said Major Bruce sternly. "Sassenach," he pronounced out clearly. "It just means Saxon, or Englishman, but that's a bad word in a large part of Scotland."

"You will very soon show the countrypeople how different you are from their picture of you." Matilda tried to comfort him. Sitting so close to him in this elegant carriage, she had been made aware as never before of the missing arm. He was so brave, this great handsome soldier; made so little ado over his stunning loss! She felt her heart becoming warm again as it had done several times before—with admiration, of course! Her sudden glow could have nothing to do with the interesting smell that clung to his person—made up, she decided, of clean linen and a warm body and perhaps some kind of spice from the soap he used. She had her mouth open to ask about his soap when she realized that such a question might reveal the direction of her thoughts, and she desisted quickly. Instead she asked a question about his great-uncle.

Major Bruce had been watching the fascinating rise and fall of color in the small face and been wondering just what had set her to blushing. However, he turned his attention to her question. "Great-uncle Willum quarreled with every member of the family, singly and in groups," he began, in the tone of one preparing to relate a lengthy tale. He was pleased to observe that his audience settled itself to listen with real interest. What a pair of babies they were! mused the major. Babes-in-the-woods, innocents! A good thing it was himself who had discovered them and taken them under his wing! When he thought of Tark—! That foul excuse for a gentleman, who had slimed his way across Europe, a disgrace to the name of Englishman! Well, Robert Bruce would see that the fellow didn't get his filthy hands on Lady Matilda!

Recollecting his audience, Bruce told about the old laird, a miserly old fellow who had gradually alienated every member of his family, and even the most determined hangers-on, until at last he moldered away in his run-down, ancient stone keep in the north of Scotland, with even the dying remnants of his clan eager to avoid him.

Matilda sighed. "It is sad, really, when one thinks of his solitary existence—"

Major Bruce denied such maudlin excesses. "That's the way the old skelpin wanted it," he said briskly. "But there's not denying he's made it mighty awkward for us."

Matilda thrilled at the thought of being part of "us." "You mean we shall find things in a mess?"

"A colossal mess," agreed the major with gruesome relish. "Also we shall have to extricate ourselves from it, because it's one thing sure, the people in the neighborhood won't help us. We'll be lucky if they don't march against the castle the moment we settle in."

"Do they know we—*you*—are coming?" she whispered, a little alarmed at the picture he was drawing.

"Oh, yes, the lawyers have informed the local minister, and the merchant, and a few of the neighboring lairds. No one sent me any welcome notes. I did send on an order—a large one—for staple food supplies, and cut logs for the fireplaces, and oil for the lamps. And I enclosed a sum of money that was more than ample to cover the damage." He pursed his lips. "That ought to give them something to stew over."

"You've been busy," said Matilda, not quite liking the cynical tone of his speech. "The large orders, and the excess of money. To say nothing of all the purchases you made yesterday." A toss of her head indicated the filled baggage wagon following the carriage.

The major looked at her with interest. "Do I detect a note of waspishness?" he inquired.

Matilda rose to the taunt. "I would have liked to help. Buying all those things—ordering supplies. . . . What did you get?" Catching his quizzical glance, she said stubbornly, "I am your chef. I have a right to know, surely, as your servant."

"Do you begin to see yourself as a member of my clan?" he teased her. "My liege woman?"

"I know my place, Major Bruce," the girl began stiffly.

"I wonder if you really do," murmured the man, so softly she did not hear him.

Robert Bruce felt it was time to change the subject, for both their sakes. "We are going to stop in Edinburgh to replenish our wardrobes with good Scottish clothing that will not bring us into ridicule with the clansmen. And, from what I am told, there are literally no amenities at the castle, so we shall have to lay in a good supply of everyday necessities. I shall rely heavily upon Fredricks and Miss Alford for guidance there."

Matilda was happier at once. "You will not be disappointed in them, Major Bruce," she said firmly. "They will fit you and your castle out as—as 'fine as fivepence!' " Glorying in his laughter, the girl went on, "Please let me help when you order the food supplies in Edinburgh, sir? Polly can bear witness that I am an excellent cook, trained over the years by my parents' French chef, Pierre!"

Polly, delighted at being drawn into the conversation by her mistress, began to praise Lady Matilda's cooking enthusiastically. Major Bruce held up one hand, his eyes sparkling with mirth.

"You have no need to convince me, Polly," he told her. "Have I not eaten one of Milady's delicious meals already, at the Cock and Pheasant? Although McLeod and I had to wait half an hour for seats at a table, so widely had the fame of Milady's cooking spread!"

Matilda wasn't sure whether he was teasing her or not, but she replied stoutly, "Pierre said I had the touch—whatever that is!—and told me I could have had a future in haute cuisine had I not been a noblewoman."

At once she regretted her idle remark, for the major's expression became sober. "Which brings me to a subject we must discuss at once," he said quietly. "You *are* a noblewoman, and it can have no happy outcome for either of us to pretend you are a cook in my kitchen." He silenced her cry of protest. "Polly, tell her that such a thing is not *convenable*, not proper, in society. You are her friend. You must convince her I am right."

Polly regarded her mistress beseechingly. "I guess the major is right, milady. Miss Alford wouldn't like it."

Even the introduction of that name did not remove the stubborn frown from Matilda's face. "If she is with us, what can be wrong? She is surely guarantee of *convenable* behavior! One could not ask for a more suitable chaperon!"

"But that is hardly the question, my dear child," said Major Bruce heavily. For some reason unfathomable to himself, he found he would like nothing better than to carry this stubborn, high-couraged little battle-maid off to his ruined castle and keep her there forever, but she was scarcely more than a child, and a runaway from her parents. No man who counted himself a gentleman would take advantage of her lovely innocence. So he said sternly, "You shall be my honored guest until we find something for you to do that will protect your good name as well as filling your reticule. Being cook for a single man is not what your family could ever condone. Your father would call me out—and rightly so."

This grim pronouncement stopped Matilda's spate of protest before it had a chance to get started. Darkly she brooded, while Polly and the major waited for her response.

"When I consider," she said at last, "what fate my parents had planned for me, I am not much moved at the thought of their grief at finding me in some man's kitchen. And it is not certain they would ever discover me in darkest Scotland, is it? But I shall wait, and discuss the problem with Miss Alford. She, at least, has always had my best interests at heart. *She* loves me.''

This speech naturally cut off dialogue, since both Polly and the major were convicted of lack of love by it. While Polly was sure Lady Matilda really knew she loved her, and was only indulging a small tantrum, the major had not even that much comfort. Of course, he didn't love the little limmer! She was plain and bossy and stubborn . . . and she had wide golden eyes that threatened to draw a man into their glowing depths and mesmerize him into forgetting the good hard common sense he'd bought so dearly—

The major caught at his rambling thoughts. *He surely was not in love with the little female!* As a soldier, an officer, of twenty-nine, he had had his normal share of experiences with the opposite sex. And behaved as a gentleman should. But this was, somehow, *different*. He scrutinized the determined little face as though seeing it for the first time.

Plain? his eyes asked his mind incredulously. That dear small oval, with the luscious soft pink lips, now delightfully pouted with stubborn resolve to get her own way. The neat straight nose, the rounded chin, above all, the glorious eyes, now half-lidded and fringed with delicate dark lashes. This girl was not plain! How could he have been so blind, mused the major, watching the soft lips. How could he have missed her special quality?

Perhaps it is like a hidden treasure, he told himself, in a mood that would normally have had him doubting his own sanity. To be revealed only to those who have the perception to recognize it?

He was snatched from these admittedly mawkish musings by the sound of the girl's voice.

"What am I to do until you have bundled me away somewhere?"

The major knew it was time to exercise his manly decisiveness. "You will stay under my care until I have found a suitable and safe place for you," he said sternly. "And in the meantime, you will remember that I am the laird."

And I hope to heaven that will hold her, he thought desperately. I can see I must be firm with her—and with myself, he added gloomily. I may have to pick a quarrel with her, he groaned, to protect her! Or yourself, gibed his soldier's mind.

It was a silent, rather unhappy group that arrived at the posting house where the major had arranged to have dinner served to his party.

Chapter Five

Edinburgh.

Matilda stared out the window of the comfortable hotel in which Robert Bruce had set up his party. The great rock loomed before her, crowned with its ancient, noble buildings. Behind her in the big bedroom, Miss Alford and Polly were emptying boxes, shaking out clothing, hanging things in the giant armoire, and gabbling meanwhile of the exciting things that had been happening during the last few days.

It seemed to Matilda that the two women had not stopped talking for one moment since the joyous reunion late last night. And now the major and Fredricks, accompanied by a much-relieved McLeod, were off purchasing clan tartans for all the members of Bruce's staff entitled to wear them—and possibly for some who were not but wanted to. For himself, the new laird had ordered the finest in his family's lovely plaids: day wear, formal evening gear, the knee socks, even the skean dhu, a small dagger that was traditional wear. Matilda tried to stifle her fears about the reception her employer, thus bedecked, might get from his not-so-loyal clansmen. She sighed and turned back to watch her governess and Polly.

Miss Alford was holding up a gray silk dress with a fetching ruffled fichu of lace. "But this is beautiful, Matilda! What good taste your major has!"

"He is not *my major*, and I think he should not have bought so many lovely gowns for me! Quite ineligible! I had thought you would support me in that judgment!"

Miss Alford sighed but did not seem too depressed. "I might have tried to do so, dear child, had I not already been given an impressive example of the major's manly decisiveness! Sergeant McLeod informed us that his master had given him a list of things he deemed Fredricks and I would need. The list was so long that the good sergeant was compelled to buy a baggage wagon to hold all the 'necessities.' Did our employer bullock you thus?" Her eyes twinkled with amusement.

"He insisted! He ignored my protests!" She hesitated, then grinned. "And since I had come away with only a single change of clothing, I let him do it."

"I imagine few could stand against Major Bruce when he gives an order," said Miss Alford. "Sergeant McLeod has been singing his praises all the way from Brighton. He tells us that the gallant and very courageous major lost his arm saving McLeod's life on the battlefield. I think the good sergeant would die for him."

"Let us hope," said Matilda with equal seriousness, "that he will not be called upon to do so. I am given to understand that the clansmen had such a dislike of the old laird that they fear and resent the coming of the new one. Moreover, he tells me that there is also a deeply rooted hatred of anything Sassenach," confided Matilda.

The three women glanced at one another anxiously. "What can we do to help the major?" asked Polly.

"It is hard to say, until we are faced with actual challenges," began Miss Alford seriously. "Still, we can all give him our loyalty and support." Catching their nods of agreement, she smiled again. "We are really becoming members of Major Bruce's clan, are we not? I must find out if all clanspeople were born to it, or if, like liege men, they could be sworn into loyal service?''

Matilda's romantic heart was touched. "I do not know why it is, since I only agreed to become his chef, but the idea of being Major Bruce's clanswoman is most attractive. If he will permit it,'' she added gloomily.

Miss Alford raised an eyebrow. "Why, what is this?'' she asked. "From the evidence presented, I should imagine Robert Bruce has adopted you as part of his family already!'' Her eye scanned the several attractive gowns in the armoire.

Matilda frowned. "Oh, he is generous to a fault! But he has already warned me that he does not think it *convenable* for me to serve in his kitchen.''

"What a sensible man!'' Miss Alford surprised Matilda by saying. "Of course, he is right.''

"But I am a good cook! I've told you how the patrons at the Cock and Pheasant clamored for my meals!''

"That is not the question,'' answered Miss Alford firmly.

Matilda wore her stubborn expression. "Oh, I know he is going on about the fact that I am too young, and nobly born, and irrelevancies of that sort. What he is refusing to admit is that I am in flight from my cruel parents and do not wish to be returned to wed that nasty Tark. You cannot say that life in the major's kitchens would be worse than a marriage to the wicked earl!''

"I am only saying that there might be other—ah—alternatives, dear child,'' soothed Miss Alford. "Why do we not practice patience and allow our good benefactor to present his plan to us when he has formulated one? I trust Major Bruce. Do not you?''

Of course, there could be only one answer to that question. Still, Miss Alford observed that her pupil had a Friday face on her, not at all compatible with the gifts and new clothing her generous employer was showering upon them all.

* * *

Within a couple of days, the new laird had done all he reasonably could in preparation for the descent upon Glenholme Castle, and the cavalcade set off for the north just after dawn of a fine morning. It seemed to the women, whose numbers were now augmented by the presence of two young maids, that theirs was an impressive caravan indeed, with its several baggage wagons, lordly carriage, coach for the servants, and smart curricle for the major's personal use. With appropriate coachmen, grooms, and outriders. A progress, indeed!

When Matilda caught sight of the rakish curricle, her heart misgave her. It looked so very *fast*! Was it possible that even an experienced whip could manage that tricksy two-wheeled carriage with only one arm? She confided her fears to McLeod, who had apparently accepted her as a member of the laird's clan.

"Can he manage it, McLeod?" she whispered, catching him as the party prepared to remount after a tasty lunch at a wayside inn.

The sergeant followed her gaze toward the dazzling little sporting carriage. "I believe so, milady," he muttered back. "In any event, I shall always be at his side, as is only right and proper."

With this, the girl had to be content, although her tender heart knew many qualms when she considered what might happen to a man with only one arm—however noble, capable, strong, and courageous he might be.

London. Portman Square.

Lord George Mountavon, looking very haggard indeed, came into his wife's drawing room just an hour before dinner. He had been, as Lady Amelia well knew, following a tantalizing clue—a glimpse Jake had reported of someone who might have been Polly, working at some wretched inn on the outskirts of London. He did not, he had informed his wife with some acerbity, intend telling the story of his ungrateful child's callous defection from duty to any official department, being very sure that word of it would immediately percolate throughout society.

There was, however, the direfully urgent matter of the earl of Tark's return to London within the week. He would be expecting—and correctly so—that the banns for his approaching marriage to Lady Matilda Mountavon would have been proclaimed. He would also be justified in assuming—alas, incorrectly!—that the wedding arrangements, for which he had agreed to stand the nonsense, would also be well in train by now.

Unfortunately the bride-to-be could not be found.

In Portman Square, fury and alarm had turned into panic. Invitations had already gone out for the small, select dinner that was to be the occasion of the announcement of the betrothal of the Right Honorable Earl of Tark to Lady Matilda Mountavon. The earl himself was due to arrive in London within two days. And still no clue as to the wretched Matilda's whereabouts!

"Where can she have gone?" raged Lord George. "She wasn't in Brighton. The old hag swore she hadn't seen her. She's got no friends; you saw to that! D'you suppose she's run off with some man?"

Lady Amelia implied that she could not care less. What worried her was the threat of social disaster hanging over her head when the guests assembled and found no fluttering bride-to-be.

"It's worse than that," said Lord George. "Tark will call in my vowels at once. We shall be ruined, penniless! Can't you understand that? She's done us in, the little slut!"

"You'd better run and tell him what's happened as soon as he gets to London," advised his wife with a sneer. "He won't enjoy learning in front of half the ton that he's been jilted by a chit of eighteen!"

"Why don't you cancel your precious dinner?" snapped

her husband. "You can always put it on again when we find her."

"Everyone in London would suspect the worst if we cancel," objected the woman crossly. "I know exactly the sort of thing they'd say—!"

"Well, *I know* what Tark's going to say," muttered her spouse, "and you'll like that less than the gabble of a few old quizzes. He'll take it as a deadly insult and ruin us! He's a vindictive devil. He'll make us a laughingstock—to say nothing of beggaring us! Where will you go when he throws us out of this house, milady?"

"Find the girl!" wailed his wife. "Question the servants again! She was always a favorite belowstairs. Gets that from your side of the family, no doubt. You always did have a penchant for barmaids!"

When they had quite exhausted themselves with graceless recriminations, the Mountavons turned their rage and fear upon the servants and the true culprit, their runaway daughter. It had at first seemed simple enough: the silly chit had probably followed her former governess to Brighton, where she was laughing at the position in which she had placed her parents. Lord George had gone off in a fine fury to seek out the governess, only to discover that the apprehensive Miss Alford had not seen her pupil since their recent parting, witnessed by most of the staff, in London. Further inquiries among the neighbors had confirmed Miss Alford's statement.

At that point, a frisson of pure terror had chilled the anger of Lord George. What if the girl had committed suicide! It seemed absurd to suspect it, but females, he was convinced, were subject to all sorts of queer vaporings and ridiculous starts. If Matilda had indeed taken her life, how would he be able to settle his debt with the earl of Tark? It had been a stroke of the greatest good fortune that the cynical nobleman had been willing to accept a green girl of no great beauty as an exchange for the enormous stack of I.O.U.'s!

In desperation, Lord George had sent out every male servant in his household, first to all the posting houses carrying traffic out of London, and then, in dreadful urgency as the time drew short, to make guarded investigations at every possible place the girl might have chosen as a refuge.

The only shred of evidence he could turn up was Jake's brief glimpse of the wench Polly. By the time Lord George had reached the Cock and Pheasant to check out the tale, however, it was the following day, and the birds, if ever they had been there, had flown. Lord George had a demeaning argument with the host's wife, a virago calling herself Mrs. Dodd, who frankly informed him he was crazy if he thought she would harbor a runaway noblewoman in her establishment.

"More like a Chelt'n'm tragedy, that is," sneered the creature. After making a number of rude suggestions in a loud voice, she called her beef-witted husband to show the gentleman off the premises.

She heaved a sigh of relief after he had gone, and stringently warned her servants to hold their tongues about the runaway debutante on pain of instant dismissal. Meanwhile Lord George was having panicky thoughts of putting a period to his own life or, failing that, of removing to the Continent rather than face the nobleman who held all his notes-of-hand.

The Mountavons now acted in a typical manner: Lord George began to try to drink himself into a lethargy; while his Lady went out and bought herself a whole new wardrobe, on credit. Thus, when the earl, much invigorated by his revels in Rome, arrived at their town house to meet his bride-to-be, he was greeted by an elaborately dressed, grim-faced female and a comatose male.

It did not take the earl long to discover the extent of the disaster. When her husband refused, or was unable, to furnish any information as to the whereabouts of Lady Matilda, the girl's mother offered, with a despairing coyness, to find a substitute.

The earl was not amused. He had finally nerved himself to enter the confounded, restricting state of matrimony for reasons that were urgent but not to be noised abroad. To find that the female who was to receive the honor of bearing his name and his heir had run away from her home to escape the distinction was unpalatable news, to say the least. The earl scanned the faces of the reprehensible parents with the coldest glance Lady Amelia had ever had to encounter.

"Have you made it known in London, in the ton, that is, that I planned to marry your daughter next week?" he challenged.

"*I* have told no one," lied the Lady Amelia.

The earl's icy stare told her what reliance he placed upon that sop to his dignity. "I am to suppose that you have made at least a token effort to find your daughter," was his next thrust.

"We have searched diligently—but to no avail," reported her ladyship. "She has disappeared without trace!"

Lord George, whom all parties had considered to be quite out of it, roused himself sufficiently to say, "Cock and Pheasant" before lapsing again into his lethargy.

"And what is *that* supposed to mean?" snarled the Earl.

Perforce, the Lady Amelia told him.

The earl at once demanded the attendance of the servant Jake, rudely advised Lady Amelia to get her disreputable gamester of a husband to bed, and closeted himself for a half hour with Jake. The upshot of this conference was a foray upon the Cock and Pheasant by the earl, accompanied by four burly grooms and Jake.

It did not take Mrs. Dodd long to get the earl's measure. A very different kettle of fish from Lord Mountavon was this damn-your-eyes nobleman! Estimating the destructive powers of the burly grooms, she quickly opened her budget to the earl.

Chapter Six

The major's party arrived at Glenholme at sunset.

After one dazzled glance around the wide green valley and
the snug little village built on either side of a small river, Matilda's eyes focused on the ancient gray stones of the castle,
at this moment warmed into soft gold by the setting sun.

At this distance, the castle did not present the ruined aspect
Matilda had expected from Major Bruce's comments. The
twin towers raised their crenellated tops against the gray stone
cliffs that guarded the castle at the rear. The massive wood-
and-iron gate was open, and the drawbridge was lowered
across the river, which had been brought around by some earlier laird to form a moat about Glenholme Castle. It was a
lovely sight, and Matilda thrilled to it. Her glance at once
flashed to the owner of this historic beauty.

Major Bruce's handsome weather-darkened face was controlled, expressionless, as he surveyed his inheritance. The
fine silver-gray eyes were slightly narrowed, but other than
that, there was no indication of his feelings. Had he ever seen
his castle before? Matilda wondered. Or was this a first view?

Being Matilda, she asked him. "Had you been here before, major?"

The big man turned slightly to get her in full view. "If,
madam, you are desirous of cementing your at-the-moment

rather shaky position in my household," he began with a wide grin that took the sting out of the pompous words, "then I must remind you that I wish to hear my full name on your lips. Always."

Matilda smiled. "Major Bruce," she said, primming it.

The man laughed, such a lovely free shout of pleasure, with his fine head thrown back on the firm, round column of his throat, that Matilda felt a strange inner trembling, quite pleasant, which she never before had experienced.

"To answer your question." The beautiful gray eyes laughed into hers. "No, I have never before seen the castle. But it is a goodly heritage . . . even in ruins."

Matilda frowned and scanned the ancient pile more carefully. Now she could discern the tumbled blocks of stone that had fallen away from parts of the outer wall, and the general air of disuse that marked the building.

"You'll restore it to its former glory," she said encouragingly. "You have told me that your relative left you a great fortune." And your recent openhandedness has confirmed it, she thought, glancing down at the modish travel outfit that the new laird had deemed proper for his temporary chef.

Before she had a chance to repeat her thanks, offered earlier, for the generosity he had shown them all, Fredricks had approached the two who stood staring over the shadowed valley.

"If I may be permitted to say so, sir, this is a noble holding," the older man said quietly. "Welcome home, Major Bruce."

The sentimental Matilda could have wept tears of gratitude at Fredrick's apt speech. Even the self-controlled Robert Bruce gave his new retainer a wide smile and a word of thanks. Then, eschewing any further sentimental weakness, the two men set about getting the train of carriages and wagons down into the valley.

The major had decided to settle into his castle before calling upon any of the local residents, either for help or in courtesy. His whole staff were well aware by this time that their new employer was a stranger in this neighborhood, the heir of a justly unpopular laird, and an Englishman to boot. Three facts that might bring overt hostility to bear against the newcomers. All the menservants agreed that the Chief—for so they had taken to calling him among themselves—was as smart as he could stare, up to any rig, and a pretty downy bird, and would have little trouble consolidating his position before making any efforts to treat with the natives. They were all aware of the major's brilliant record on the Continent, but of course he had been fighting for England, which would not particularly endear him to the present company!

The small cavalcade wound its way down the hill and through the village on its way to the castle. Oddly enough, Matilda thought, there was no one out along the road to witness their arrival. Had the dwindling population finally disappeared? Then she caught just a flicker of movement between two of the cottages, and a quick closer look revealed a small boy disappearing into a mass of overgrown shrubbery.

"They do not keep their homes up very smartly," she remarked, feeling somehow that the total ignoring of the new laird was a hurtful thing. *The cut direct.*

The major shrugged. "They have had little enough in the way of encouragement, I am thinking," he said slowly. "Never a groat spent to keep up anything. The old laird did not set them much of an example."

"You will do so," averred the girl stoutly.

The man scrutinized the small, intent countenance. "You really want me to make a success of this venture, do you not?" he asked gently.

"Of course, I do! And you will!"

"I am not sure I wish to," admitted the major. "So much hostility! So difficult a task! My men-at-law have urged me to offer the place for sale and cut my losses. They fear the whole sum of the Glenholme fortune will be wasted restoring a drafty old castle no one wants to live in.''

This distinctly gloomy view of the situation gave Matilda pause. She glanced again out the window at the huge stone pile they were approaching. It did look run-down, she decided. How much work would it take to restore it to its former grandeur? And who would do the work? Unless he could enlist the help of the men in the community, the major would have to import laborers from elsewhere, no doubt at great expense. And no doubt, either, that such a course would further exacerbate the angry resentment of the local citizens! They would declare themselves unwilling to work for the Englishman—and then get into a fury because he was hiring outsiders at a good wage! Were all men irrational?

Matilda let her eyes wander over the big man beside her in the carriage. It seemed plain to her that he would not be able to move heavy blocks of stone, nor take part in whatever other repair work might be needed. One arm would hardly be enough for such work, would it? And how this big, strong competent man must hate his disability! She felt a resurgence of the partisan emotion she had noticed in herself on several earlier occasions. It seemed suddenly very important that no one should make fun of this man, or taunt him about his lost limb. She turned to face him, not yet sure what words of encouragement she would offer, but eager to voice them.

He was staring out at the castle, old and strong and glowing in the golden sunset. ''It is a lovely holding,'' he mused, in the deepest voice she had heard him use. His stern soldier's face was strangely vulnerable. The girl's heart beat once, powerfully, out of rhythm. She *had* to speak!

''*Major!*''

She lifted an encouraging countenance to meet his inquiring gaze. ''Major Robert Bruce will succeed in restoring his

lovely ancestral home to its original strength and beauty,''
she said firmly.

And loved the warm smile with which he greeted her af-
firmation of faith.

In the event, the major and his men between them made a
heartwarming occasion of the homecoming. Although the
state of neglect they found in all the rooms, the obvious lack
of care for the fine old furniture, tapestries, silver and china,
appalled them all, the servants immediately set to work to
light fires in the kitchen and the Great Hall.

When Miss Alford bustled in behind Matilda to assess the
resources of the Glenholme kitchens, the good dame uttered
a cry of horror. All eyes immediately focused upon her. She
was pointing a trembling finger at the huge open fireplace,
blackened and grease-stained and crossed by a hand-turned
spit and cranes for cooking pots.

"A relic of the Dark Ages!" she groaned. "How can you
expect us to cook upon—within—that monstrosity!"

The menservants hid grins as the major strolled over and
assessed the primitive resource. Finally, when the servants
were nearly bursting with amusement, he nodded.

"Rather primitive, I admit. But, in the meantime, there is
always that other monstrosity." He pointed to a small stove
in another part of the kitchen. "Will it be adequate for the
preparation of our meager repasts until I can have a better one
freighted in?"

At the look on Miss Alford's face, the servants burst into
laughter. The governess glanced around at the merry countenances, and a slow smile lightened her features. "I am behaving very housewifely, am I not?" she chided herself. "But
if these are the implements the old laird cooked on, I begin
to see reasons for his sour attitude. One can only hope all the
kitchen maids will consent to remain!" and she stared around
at the dirty, cobwebby kitchen with scorn.

The major faced them with such an expression of pleading apprehension on his dark, handsome face that the three kitchen maids, headed by Polly, were quick to assure him that they'd stay "if it killed them!"—with sideways glances at the admiring males.

Matilda grinned. Intentionally or not, dear Alford had just given the wily major a chance to add the active loyalty of the female servants to that of the major's besotted male retainers. Matilda hugged herself to contain the bubbling pride and admiration she, too, felt for that tall, handsome soldier. Nothing must be allowed to destroy his pride and pleasure in his inheritance! With this in mind, she moved quietly around the kitchen, recruiting helpers, assigning tasks, directing the placement of the supplies the men were already bringing in.

Oil from the supply wagons was unpacked for the new lamps they had brought, and while the men were carrying in food and new bedding, the women, led by a very determined Miss Alford, began to wash pots and pans for Matilda's use in cooking a hearty, restorative meal upon the old stove.

From her position at the stone sink, washing the dishes, Miss Alford continued to make her mock protests. First she held up a large and very dirty dinner plate that did not look as though it had ever felt the touch of soap or water. She blew on it, and a large puff of dust arose. "I dread the thought of eating from any of these dusty dishes!" she declared. "The former laird may well have choked to death!"

This feeble joke set the maids to giggling again, and preparations for dinner proceeded in an atmosphere of great good humor. Within a reasonably short time, Matilda had a hot, tasty meal ready to serve on a giant kitchen table freshly washed by Polly. The new laird, firmly refusing to stand upon ceremony or to allow anyone else to do so, commanded them all to sit down with him around the board and satisfy their hunger.

Then all the lamps were filled and lighted, and a tentative

exploration of the ground floor of the huge building was begun. It was soon evident that much hard work would have to be done before any degree of civilized comfort could be attained. As it grew dark, the major designated a large room, which was two steps up from the Great Hall and to one side, as the Ladies' Bower. He had the men set up cots there and commanded the women to get some rest, since they had worked hard and well and would need to be ready to do more of the same on the morrow. He then led his men, who now seemed to consider themselves his private army, back to the kitchen, where trundle beds and cots were quickly set up amid a good deal of laughter.

Listening to the distant sounds of mirth, Miss Alford nodded with satisfaction. "He's really a born leader, isn't he, my dear? No wonder he won those medals! I'm convinced your major can handle anything!"

Matilda, who had had her mouth open to inquire about the medals, closed it after those last words. *Her major?* It had such a cozy ring to it! As she tried to get to sleep on the hard, narrow cot, Matilda wondered what the response of the villagers would be to the new laird, Sassenach as he undoubtedly was. Could even he win these dour, opinionated Scotspeople over to his side, as he had won his new menservants, and the maids, and Polly and Miss Alford, and Fredricks? *And especially yourself!* said a small inner voice. Lying in the dusty Ladies' Bower, feeling the searching chill of night that penetrated even through the new warm blankets the major had supplied, Matilda prayed very fervently that the major would win his battle.

Chapter Seven

During the next three days, Matilda worked as she had never done before, even during the hectic days in the kitchen of the Cock and Pheasant. So, too, did everyone else at Castle Glenholme. Fredricks and Miss Alford, long accustomed to the proclivity of London servants to do as little as they could safely get away with, watched and marveled. Not only was a great deal of heavy work being accomplished, but spirits were high in the servants' quarters.

Miss Alford, surveying the smaller dining room with a view to providing a proper place for the laird, noted the cobweb-festooned walls, beams, and tapestries, and shuddered delicately. "Never have I seen such neglect in a gentleman's residence! Yet the servants, instead of grumbling as I would have expected, appear to regard the disgusting mess as a challenge, and the old ruin as their own special place. It is odd, Fredricks."

"Major Bruce has them all considering themselves his liege men and women—even your Polly," chuckled the old man. "But the castle is not really such a ruin, Miss Alford. I've been over it carefully with the laird. He admitted he needed my special knowledge, and I was glad to oblige," Fredricks added complacently.

The major enlarges us all, thought the governess. No wonder the servants are devoted to him! How does he do it? For the major hadn't a great deal to say. He insisted upon taking a full share in the labor of restoration, working beside his men, a large sturdy figure in his kilt, his hard-muscled torso covered by a clean white linen shirt. McLeod had constituted himself the major's valet as well as his sergeant-at-arms and took pride in keeping his master looking every inch the officer, no matter what kind of work they were engaged in.

Matilda had observed Robert Bruce's success with admiration and pleasure. Her earlier fears began to recede; she allowed her hopes for the future—for herself as well as for him—to rise again. It was obvious that everyone on the staff took as great a pride in their laird as did McLeod. The major was so pleasant and even in temper, so skillful in action, that Matilda was forced to revise her earlier judgment as to his ability. He lifted his end of a heavy table with the same quiet competence he used in helping to lower the dust-laden, faded tapestries for later cleaning.

He was meticulous about the disposal of daily trash and of the worm-eaten furniture and bedraggled linens he wished to discard. He had made a firm rule that nothing was to be thrown into the moat, as it would contaminate the river for the village downstream. Instead, wagons full of rejected objects were driven to a deep ravine behind the castle and dumped there. While some of the men grumbled, they were actually proud of the way the castle was beginning to look. And the stables! The major had decided they were to be rebuilt, with every device for proper housing and care of his splendid animals. It now appeared that no trouble was too great for the grooms, if it added to the comfort of the major's noble beasts. Never had Matilda seen such shining coats, such proudly tossed manes, such fine, dark liquid eyes, even in London at the hour of promenade in the park!

The laird also insisted upon his staff eating full and regular meals and continued to take his place at the head of the big servants' table in the kitchen.

"An army marches upon its stomach," he informed Matilda, "and thanks to your excellent cuisine, we are marching very well!"

When Miss Alford, glorying in her role as housekeeper for this noble residence, gently hinted that Milord's dignity might be better served if he held his state in the smaller dining hall— now clean and polished—the laird responded to her nudging with his wide, white smile.

"When we are well established in our new home, it will be time enough for me to flaunt my rank," he said. "At this moment, I am building, Miss Alford. Strengthening foundations."

Miss Alford could not understand this last remark, since the laird had given the dungeons and storage caverns beneath the castle only the most superficial attention. Was he now working down there? She shuddered at the thought, although Fredricks had already told her that the dungeons would be ideal for the storage of wines and stronger liquors.

Matilda, however, who was shamelessly eavesdropping on the conversation, thought she understood. For, in spite of the really remarkable load of work the servants had had to cope with, they appeared proud of themselves rather than resentful at the laird's demands. He was building loyalties.

Every day wagons full of furniture, carpets, dishes, and utensils arrived from Edinburgh, including the promised new stove, a massive thing that had six men panting and groaning during its installation. Instead of rebelling, however, they had cheekily informed Miss Matilda that they'd expect something really toothsome from the new ovens. Then they proceeded to tease the laird that he would have to resurface the road to the castle next, before it was worn down to China with all these comings and goings! Since they continued to unload the wares with hearty goodwill and pride, boasting to the

Edinburgh carters of the grandeur and comfort of the castle, their master made no objection to their joking. He had apparently no fears for his own consequence; the friendly teasing did not bother him at all. In fact, he gave as good or better than he got.

To the servants' delight, he had established well-furnished quarters for both men and women, with bathing rooms adjoining. There was also a suite each for Miss Alford and Fredricks, and a charming room for his chef in the South Tower. Matilda was privately of the opinion that none of the laird's people, herself included, had ever enjoyed finer accommodations.

And yet her heart was troubled at his manner toward herself. Unfailingly kind, sharing many a small jest or interesting problem with her, still the major did not permit anything of a *personal* nature to enter their discussions. Could it be, the girl thought despairingly, that the special interest he appeared to feel in his chef had been only his natural courtesy toward any woman? Matilda carefully watched his behavior to Miss Alford. Was it the same as his attitude toward herself? Courteous, yes; never condescending. But did the smile he directed at Miss Alford have the special warmth—did his eyes, when he looked at his housekeeper, hold the friendly sparkle with which he observed Matilda?

She realized that she had to know for sure. Not knowing was too painful.

And then Polly passed on some information concerning the laird's chef that seemed to threaten to destroy all her hopes, as well as bringing to an end her residence at Glenholme Castle. Reminding herself that her name meant "mighty battle-maid," the girl resolved to challenge the major that very morning. This battle plan was implemented by the appearance of the soldier himself in the kitchen.

Unaware of the coming battle, the major, with a mysterious air, invited his chef to accompany him to the South Tower

62

for a tour of inspection. At her rather severe nod of assent, he led her past the room she was presently using on the ground floor, up the curving stairway to the Ladies' Bower, a spacious suite at the top of the building, with a magnificent view of the valley and the mountains.

However dazzling it might be, the view could not hold Matilda's attention as she took in what had been done to the rooms. They had been, so the legend ran, the favored abode of the daughters of the family, or of new brides to the house. Now, by the laird's command, they had been made fresh and charmingly decorated and furnished for—whom?

Oh, he cannot be thinking of getting married! was Matilda's first despairing thought. To some woman in London?

He just stood there, her great handsome soldier, grinning like a schoolboy.

"These are your new quarters, Matilda," he said. And waited for her approval, her thanks, her delight.

Curiously enough, this amazing announcement, and the beauty and comfort of the rooms, did nothing to restore Matilda's composure. Rather it plunged her into acute distress. She remembered the information Polly had passed on. Why had the laird made just this gesture to his cook at this moment? She faced him, her expression forbidding.

"I do not understand what is happening here, Major Bruce," she began. "I am informed by Polly that you have instructed her and the other kitchen maids that I am not to be allowed to do any more of the work after today."

"You have enough to do, teaching them your skills, sharing your knowledge, superintending their work," the man answered, frowning a little at her cold reception of his efforts in preparing her rooms. He had thought the girl would be *aux anges*! Where had he gone wrong? Worried, disappointed, he continued, very much the-laird-on-his-high-horse, "I cannot have it noised abroad in Glenholme village that the Lady Matilda Mountavon drudges in my kitchen."

63

"But I *enjoy* doing it!" the girl protested. Did the stupid man not realize that her work in his kitchen was her reason, her only excuse, for remaining in his household? She made a desperate effort to inform him of her sentiments. "I feel like . . . *one of your clan!*" If that doesn't tell him how much I like him, nothing will! she thought, both embarrassed and relieved that she had made all clear at last. Her great solemn eyes beseeched him to understand.

Major Bruce had never been a ladies' man. He had been too busy all his life, first at school, and then in the army and under Wellington's command, to have much opportunity to learn the skills of a dashing beau. Decent manners, yes; he granted himself that much. But he had never been a womanizer, or even much in the company of ladies. He had to admit to himself that this small, maddening female had got him further off-balance and on the defensive than all of Napoleon's army had ever managed to do. At war, the major knew who his enemies were and how best to deal with them. But here, in this massive old castle he was coming to love, facing a brave-hearted, sweet, generous, delicious little woman who definitely should not be part of his bachelor household, he was completely at a loss.

He knew now that he should never have permitted her to accompany him from London, after he had realized her quality. Certainly he should have sent her back to her parents as soon as he discovered the true state of affairs. *But that was the rub!* The true state of affairs was that this lovely girl was in real danger of being sold to a licentious beast by her cold-hearted parents, who neither valued nor deserved so darling a daughter. But they *were* her parents, and therefore their decision as to her future could not be set aside or even argued. *The Laird of Glenholme could lose his little love, or he could keep her and see her good name irrevocably ruined.* For, of course, her father would raise hell.

Which was it to be? The man lost himself in dark forebodings.

During this unflattering delay in responding to her eager plea, Matilda's feelings were changing from beseeching adoration to righteous anger. Was this the way a gallant soldier responded to a *declaration*?

"Major Bruce! You are not paying attention to me! *Major Bruce!*"

The imperious little voice broke through his preoccupation. Focusing upon the flushed, petulant small countenance, the major set his jaw in an expression McLeod would immediately have recognized. It was the major's fighting-man-in-action expression, every instinct and skill focused on successful mastery of the situation. So, she wanted him to pay attention to her, did she? His silver eyes narrowed dangerously. Her soft rosy lips were pursed in that maddeningly desirable pout as she said his name. *Kissing-shaped!* That particular gesture had haunted him since first he beheld those red lips framing his name. It was too much for a soldier to endure. Bending toward the little witch, he pressed his own lips hard against that tantalizing softness. And pressed. And pressed . . .

His senses reeled. Instead of falling back, or protesting, or trying to remove herself, the little female had actually caught at his shoulders to steady herself against the pressure of his mouth! She *liked* it! Silver-gray eyes, unconsciously closed during the attack, flew open to meet a pair of glowing sherry-brown eyes staring into his. Slightly crossed, it must be admitted, with the effort to focus on his own intent gaze.

The major raised his head, breathing with some difficulty.

He discerned that the girl was suffering the same trouble. However, she recovered her breath more quickly than he did. Her voice reached him softly.

"That was . . . wonderful. Will you . . . do it again, please?"

The major caught at self-control with every ounce of will-power he possessed. Unfortunately his hard arm also had caught at the lovely girl, clasping her soft warmth to his chest, and his willpower gave up without a struggle. He groaned deeply.

"I like it when you do that," confided Matilda shyly, from her position close against his body. "It makes me tingle."

The major groaned again and kissed those sweet red lips. This time it was even better than before—if that was possible, the dazzled soldier thought.

"This really will not do," he gasped. "We must sit down—talk—there is so much to discuss—important matters—" He was babbling, and he knew it. But what was a man to do, with a soft, warm female pressed against him, and a pair of the loveliest eyes he had ever seen fixed on his face with a look that set his blood aflame!

The girl was regarding him with such tenderness that the major had to catch another deep breath.

"Matilda! *Merielle!* I mean it! We must sit down!" Or I may fall down, his muscles warned him.

The girl could understand the necessity. When her major spoke the name she had always wished to hear, her knees were assailed with a sudden weakness. But there was an obstacle.

"I cannot sit down while you are holding me to you so tightly," she explained. "Not that I do not enjoy the position! In fact, I am sure I prefer it to sitting down—except perhaps on your knee?" she offered hopefully.

The major, sore beset, groaned again.

This time his distress penetrated the rosy glow in which Matilda had been luxuriating since his first kiss. Was her wonderful soldier feeling ill? Gently she untangled their bodies and walked over to seat herself on a pretty little sofa—just a comfortable fit for two, she thought.

The major, staring with glassy eyes, found himself an

armchair at a safe distance, took out his spotless kerchief, and dabbed at his brow.

It seemed there was to be no escape for him. He really could not be expected to give up this darling girl.

"I really enjoyed that," Matilda was reassuring him. "When may we do it again?" She was regarding him with dazzled eyes, her expression remarkably like the one on his own face.

The major recognized the coup de grace when he received it.

"I shall marry you as soon as it can be arranged, Merielle," he managed to say. It was the proper—the only—correct behavior, he told himself, drinking in the delighted glow that began to illuminate the girl's face. Anyone would agree that he had compromised her. . . . It was his obvious duty. . . . That it was the one thing above all others that he wished to do must not be permitted to influence his thinking. *Thinking!* the soldier groaned silently. I haven't thought straight for the last half hour! Heaven help me to bring this imbroglio to a decent conclusion! To be fair to my darling girl! I'm committed now—and I would not have it any other way!

He became conscious that the girl was watching him with anxious, wondering eyes. What an oaf he was! This should have been a perfect moment for her. He summoned up a smile.

"You do wish to marry me, my darling?" he asked softly, rising and striding over to her sofa.

"Oh, yes!" gasped Matilda, horrified that there might have been any doubt. "Whenever you say!"

The gallant soldier helped her gently to her feet and kissed her chastely on the brow. He could not take a chance on what a more fervent caress would do to his shattered control.

"All will take place in good time—when I have completed the arrangements—in the proper order—with all due attention

67

to detail . . . '' He was babbling again, but he couldn't help it. Waterloo had been child's play to this encounter. The major hoped to heaven he could solve the unsolvable: marry his darling with not the faintest slur upon her good name; appease her greedy parents—Thanks to one miserly old Scotsman, he had enough money for that!

In the meantime, his lovely girl must not be allowed to worry. The important thing to remember was that he had lighted upon the perfect way of protecting his little love. (To say nothing, he reminded himself, of turning his own life into a heaven on earth, a Garden of Eden, a paradise—) He caught himself up sternly. This was not the time for romantic, sentimental weakness! He had just thrown down the gauntlet to fate, and to Lord Mountavon. A battle gage is final, even if given in the absence of the enemy. He made the mistake of staring down into the wide, lovely eyes trained so eagerly upon his countenance. He caught at his distracted thoughts. He had just set out to thwart two noblemen, either of whom would have him killed without scruple if they suspected he was in a fair way of foiling their nefarious plot.

And he had a castle to restore!

A reluctant, widening grin spread across the major's lips. He smiled down into the lovely face turned so trustingly up to his.

"We are going to have a busy time during these next few weeks, my little one," he said softly, and hugged her to him.

At this moment, Matilda could not be bothered with the days to come. She had just become engaged!

"I think I should like you to kiss me now, *Major Bruce*," she said firmly. Surely that was comme il faut!

"You are doing it again!" groaned the hapless soldier, drawn to that delicious rosy pout as to a magnet. He then demonstrated, to the complete satisfaction of both parties involved, that one strong arm can anchor a small body to a large one very effectively.

68

Chapter Eight

The following morning Matilda waited for the laird to announce their forthcoming marriage. True, he had been very quiet after their solemnly passionate embrace, conducting her without digression to her original room at the foot of the Tower and leaving her there with one chaste, brief kiss upon her forehead. Matilda knew herself to be no connoisseur of kisses, having had so few—and none of them from members of the opposite sex. In fact, now that she thought about it, the only person who had ever kissed her was Miss Alford.

Matilda wondered if the effect of those firm contacts of lip with lip had been as impressive to Major Bruce as they had been to her. It was possible, no, certain, that such a handsome, desirable male had been permitted to take and give many kisses during the course of his adult life—and not with his governess! Thinking of governesses, as she was unaccountably doing, Matilda wondered whether the major would speak to Miss Alford first, as to one in loco parentis, or whether he would, in true lairdly fashion, announce the news to the whole staff at dinner.

He did neither.

Though his manner to her was gentle and courteous as ever, there was no particularity of attention, no ardent glance, no murmured word of endearment.

As the hours passed, Matilda's happiness drained away, and she became so pale and listless that Miss Alford, alarmed, prescribed a dose of oil and honey. Matilda naturally refused this nauseating brew with every sign of revulsion. Miss Alford then threatened to consult the laird. This was the final straw.

"I wish you," Matilda retorted with surprising bitterness, "success in dealing with such an insensitive and callous person!"

Miss Alford's eyes opened wide. Was the child *really* ill? Such venom against a man who had behaved, in Miss Alford's opinion, with more than courtesy to her young charge! She began to say so. Matilda broke into tears and ran off to her new room.

Why she went there was not clear to the girl. Perhaps she wished to assure herself that the major, however remote and cool in his manner today, had been thrillingly ardent yesterday.

This was another mistake. The dainty new furniture, the delicate fabrics, all the charming touches, did nothing to restore Matilda's composure. Rather, they made her distress more painful. What could have happened during the night to change the major's mind? Had she done something to give her soldier second thoughts? Why, she brooded, did he kiss me if he does not intend to make me his wife? For after all, it had been the major who had mentioned marriage.

Sunk in these melancholy reflections, Matilda at first missed the announcement of the attack upon the castle. Warning of the advance was given to the major by Sergeant McLeod, who had, upon the arrival of the major's household at Glenholme, immediately set up a sentry patrol with the full agreement of the English servants. No tellin' what'll happen in these savage parts, they grinned, only half joking. The servants hired in Edinburgh smugly agreed.

The man now on duty reported that two large wagons,

crowded with men, were coming up the road at a steady pace. Within three minutes of the warning, every able-bodied male within the walls was alerted to the imminent arrival of a large, possibly hostile force. They took their places out of sight behind the wall with enthusiasm; it was a refreshing break in the day's work. Major Bruce strolled down to stand just outside the great stone arch, which contained the wooden, iron-bound gates to the castle and the mechanism for the drawbridge. It was noted with admiration that the major was his usual imperturbable self, not quite smiling, standing tall but relaxed outside his castle.

"Jus' like a real laird," whispered one man.

"He *is* the laird," growled McLeod, "an' don't you ferget it!"

The wagons halted at the far side of the river-moat, now flowing free and swift thanks to the major's instructions. He scrutinized the enemy. The driver of the foremost wagon was a small fat man with a smile pasted upon a wary face. Seated next to him on the wooden seat was a gaunt man dressed in clerical black with a crisp white stock and a censorious but uncomfortable frown. Behind them, the second wagon was full of roughly dressed men, every one of whom had his gaze fastened upon the large, well-muscled figure in the working kilt and white shirt standing with powerful legs astride and looking completely master of the place and the situation. Not an eye missed the empty sleeve neatly pinned at one side of the broad chest. And even at the distance imposed by the drawbridge, not one missed the steely glint in the strange light eyes.

Somehow the man they'd come to taunt and jostle did not fit the image merchant Wallace had given them of a jumped-up, foppish Sassenach. Standing alone in the sunlight beneath his ancient arch, he more closely resembled the heroic figures in Scottish history; so at least thought the Reverend George Cameron, already uneasy at his part in this sortie. He

71

was having second thoughts about the whole undertaking, and wondered why he had permitted the bullheaded storekeeper to coax him into this gesture against the new owner. He had hoped by his presence to keep the situation in hand and prevent violence. As he absorbed the truly quelling glance the soldier was giving them, Cameron wondered whose violence he might need to control. And indeed the Englishman was within his legal rights and had offered no offense to decency or good order—so far. The clergyman set his mouth with distaste for the situation Wallace had created.

The youngest of the wagonload of men, fifteen-year-old Colin Wallace, described the scene to his mother later. "The Sassenach wasna' angry, exactly, but we men knew better than to speak out o' turn. All but Dad, that is."

His mother groaned with exasperation, shaking her head. "Tell me!" she commanded.

Enthusiastically he did so. Merchant Wallace had ignored the steady, enigmatic scrutiny that held his companions silent.

"You'll be the new owner, then?" he called out. He did not give the Sassenach he had come to intimidate the courtesy of a title.

"I am Robert Bruce," the officer vouchsafed quietly.

Thanks to the grapevine, they all knew that, and that the fellow had been a major in Wellington's army. Also that he had given Wallace a substantial order and accompanied it with more than enough money to pay for it—at normal rates. Of course, Wallace had assured them in the tavern the previous evening, you always charge the nobs more! But this particular nob did not seem to be fitting into merchant Wallace's pattern. For one thing, that "Robert Bruce," spoken in the new owner's deep voice, had a fine, familiar Scottish ring to it, a faint and authentic rolling of the *r*'s. And for another, that steel-hard glance did not suggest the easygoing, gullible ninnyhammer Wallace had promised.

The villagers began to wonder what they were doing here and to wish they had come in a rather different spirit. Yet the big man hadn't said a word beyond his name or made a hostile gesture. Even more strangely, the fact that he had only one arm did not at all diminish him. After the first glance, they had hardly been aware of it.

Wallace the insensitive rushed on his doom. "Well, man, we've come to put you straight," he began, loud-voiced and bullying.

The Reverend Cameron frowned. The merchant was behaving very much like the Gadarene swine referred to in the Good Book, who, taken over by demons, rushed violently toward their own destruction. He resolved to take that text as the subject for his sermon the following Sunday. At the moment, he was obliged to content himself with a sour look at his blabber-mouthed companion. Couldn't Wallace recognize quality when he saw it?

The merchant was plunging on. "The money you sent for the supplies you ordered," he jerked his hand at the crates and boxes in the bed of the wagon, "was not enough, Bruce," he sneered. "Are ye like the auld man, then? Quick wi' the orders an' slow wi' the bawbees?"

The minister gasped. There was even a shocked murmur from Wallace's friends and customers in the second wagon. But the merchant, his jeering gaze fixed upon the face of the major, now experienced a sudden sharp twinge of doubt. Instead of the timid apology or outright fear he had expected to see upon the new owner's countenance, Wallace was chilled to perceive the narrow-eyed, hard wariness of a man about to fight. With the dismayed conviction that he'd just run out of luck, Wallace cravenly abandoned his original rash plan to engage in a battle of words with the Englishman. In a completely different tone of voice, he said, turning to nod at the cleric beside him, "This gentleman is the Reverend George

Cameron, our esteemed presbyter—that is, our minister. He had come to—er—bid you welcome to our valley. Sir.''

This was such a shameless about-face that the minister shot a shocked and disapproving glance at the merchant before bowing his head in formal greeting. He then said, rather tight-lipped, "I bid you welcome, Major Bruce.''

And he would definitely preach on the subject of the Gadarene swine next Sabbath, with sharp reference to the sins of pride, presumption, and pure knuckleheaded stupidity. He only hoped his belated and grudging courtesy would be enough to satisfy the soldier.

The major was taking a moment to consider this odd reversal of strategy. What was the purpose behind this rather ridiculous charade? Was the sudden change part of a devious scheme or merely the result of inept bullying and cowardice upon the part of the merchant and innate kindness in the minister? Were they testing the enemy? It seemed more like an attempt to play up the new boy, thought the major, recalling his own childhood at school.

Still, he was not about to reject the hand of friendship, however reluctantly offered. He was well aware that he had not been given the title of laird. So, they did not plan to admit him to his full and proper position in the community? At this moment, Major Bruce thought grimly, he did not want any favors from men who had come to show their hostility to his arrival.

Or had they? the astute campaigner in him queried. The only attack so far had come from Wallace, and he had retracted it in haste at the first sign of trouble. And the minister, even if compelled to do so in common courtesy by his cowardly companion, had extended a firm welcome. The major smiled, bowed, and said, "Thank you for your welcome, Dr. Cameron.'' Then he glanced beyond the two men in the front wagon, raking his eyes over the crowd in the other vehicle. They didn't look very angry, or even particularly hostile;

rather, they seemed curious, he thought, but trying hard to conceal it. The faintest of smiles tugged at the major's firm lips.

"You, Wallace, will get all that you deserve," he said, with a feral grin that sent shivers over several of his audience. He raised his one hand in a casual gesture.

Out from behind the wall marched the major's private army, all of them neat and trim in their working kilts and white shirts. The swing of those kilts as they moved into place behind the major impressed even Matilda, who, with the other women, watched with bated breath from within the Great Hall.

It was obvious that the unexpected appearance of the major's troops had shocked the villagers. His self-control in a difficult situation had impressed them, but this development placed him in a professional category far outside their limited experience.

Except for one young man. He scrambled out of the second wagon and limped quickly toward the merchant. "Have ye no sense, Wallace? Insultin' the major on his own ground? D'ye want to bring total ruin to the valley?" He drew himself up awkwardly and saluted the grim-faced major. "I'll get them away quietly, sir," he muttered, his face red with embarrassment.

The major scrutinized the peacemaker with interest.

"That was a very professional, learned-on-the-field-of-battle salute, sir," he commented quietly.

An unreadable expression briefly twisted the young man's face. "I served against Napoleon, sir, until I was invalided home."

The major stood straighter and returned the salute. "You served—?" he began.

"He was in London, making purchases for our business here, when he had one too many in a pub and found he'd taken the King's shilling when he woke up," snarled Wallace, all his grievances once more recalled.

And here's a fine kettle of fish, thought the major. *How* do I get around that one? His smile became very gentle. He took a pace forward, held out his hand. His only hand.

"As one veteran to another?" he asked, his eyes fixed on the face of the young man. "May I know your name?"

No one breathed, so intense was the moment.

Finally, his own gaze firmly held by the major's, the young man reached out and clasped the offered hand. "I'm Ian Wallace," he managed through a tight throat.

"And you served as purchasing agent for your father," mused the major. "Now, that sort of experience, with your training as a soldier, should make you just the man I am looking for," he said with a decisive nod.

"You are looking for . . . " repeated Ian Wallace, for once quite forgetting his injuries at this tantalizing idea.

The major smiled again. "I have great need of a factor here at the castle. My excellent butler, Fredricks, has far too much to do restoring order in the household to be burdened with estate matters. But you, Wallace, have evidently been trusted to carry out the duties of factor for your father. I believe that no one present can deny that Castle Glenholme needs—a business administrator?" He included them all, for the first time, in the warmth of his open smile. Raising his voice above the murmur of laughter and wry comments, he continued, "You may also be aware that my Great-Uncle Willum died a very wealthy man. As the presbyter will tell you—and probably has upon numerous occasions—" (this got another laugh, and even a prim smile from the Reverend Cameron)— "*he could not take it with him.* So, perforce, it came to me. And with it, I am told, a great many debts. It shall be your unenviable task, Ian Wallace, if you accept it, to see to the settling of all outstanding debts in the neighborhood, and the subsequent handling of the estate's affairs. That is, if your father can spare you?''

Spare him? thought the dazzled soldier. The major was the first person who had seemed to need him since his inglorious return, wounded and bitter, from a war he hadn't intended to fight in! His minatory glance at the elder Wallace told the merchant exactly what his son's sentiments were. Himself dazed by the turn of events, Wallace began to babble his willingness to spare his older son at once to be the major's factor.

"Thank you, Major Bruce," said Ian quietly.

"You will not be disappointed, major," added Cameron. "Ian was a bright student and quick to pick up information and skills."

"And now, Mr. Wallace," said the new factor briskly, "you've some supplies to deliver at the castle, I believe."

Every man present grinned at the look of astonishment and annoyance that crossed the merchant's face at his son's tone.

"Better be sure he pays you," advised the major, sotto voce. "This establishment's got a bad name in the district, Mr. Wallace."

That set them all off. Even the maids, clustering with Matilda and Miss Alford just within the open doors of the Great Hall, were drawn into the delighted roar that followed the major's final quip. Miss Alford shook her head in appreciation.

"He's a wonder, your major," she sighed. "Up to every trick in the book—and invents his own when he needs to!"

Matilda said grimly, "I think I must talk with you, dear Alford, on a matter of great importance—" Her voice broke over the final word, and she sobbed once.

The governess peered at her dear pupil with a worried frown. "What is it, child? Are you ready to tell me?"

"I believe I must, Alford. But perhaps it had better be this evening, when the problems of the castle are not so pressing."

Miss Alford nodded, and they went about their tasks.

The laird was proceeding with his affairs very nicely. He had hardly had to mention that he could use a few competent workers to staff the castle and home farm, when every man in the second wagon hurried down to volunteer. The major smiled at Ian Wallace. "You know these men better than I do, factor. It is your responsibility to hire the ones we can use."

With matters so well in hand, the major invited the Reverend Cameron to dinner the following night. Glancing at the merchant busily superintending the unloading of the supplies in the courtyard beside the kitchen door, he added, "Without your loyal friend, I am afraid."

George Cameron smiled. He knew the major had not missed the differences in attitude and opinion expressed between the two men.

"He would not come if you did invite him. It would offend his sense of propriety," the cleric instructed him. "His son may serve you to the father's great satisfaction. And he will make very sure he has the last jot and tittle of the sums you or your great-uncle owe him. But fraternize at your table he will not. It would not be suitable."

"Thank you for this information," said the major, concealing a grin. The story of his instruction in local customs would, of course, filter through the village. It would be a small victory for the merchant—the newcomer's put-down—and would serve to soothe his ruffled dignity.

One more hurdle taken successfully, Bruce decided. Perhaps he might even come out of this imbroglio with a well-run home, a contented staff, and a few friends. As to a wife . . . He knew he ought to put that tantalizing thought aside for a quieter, less stressful moment. What kind of mooncalf was the knowledgeable Major Bruce turning into, he asked himself with bitter mockery, that he could seriously consider asking a girl young enough to be his daughter, a girl, moreover, of noble birth, to be his wife? Yet he had asked her, and had found himself dizzy with delight at her ardent response. The child was infatuated with his position, perhaps—or was it that she, with her tender compassion, felt pity for his dreadful injury? The man set his jaw against that thought. It seemed he wanted her any way he could get her—infatuated or pitying!

Yet in the cold light of this new day, he knew he must face all the hazards of the situation. What if Matilda's father refused to permit the match? The fortune he had inherited from Willum Bruce might not be enough to cover Mountavon's losses. Even if he did bail the gamester out this time, what of the future? Did he wish to go on until he, too, was reduced to penury? Was he willing to give up all this, his heritage, to permit a conscienceless parent to fritter away his life gambling?

What else could he do? A furtive marriage ceremony was not what he wanted for his lovely girl. Yet he could not let her go back, unshielded, to her callous parents. Miss Alford could not protect Matilda from the Mountavons' wrath; nor did she have the means to keep the girl in the style to which Major Bruce would like to accustom her. Then, must he let her go?

No! He wanted her! There could be no doubt of that. And, at the moment, she wanted him. But what if she decided later, when her first adolescent infatuation had worn off, that she wanted a younger man? A whole man? The thought of having her and then losing her brought so sharp a pain that the major caught his breath.

Enough! Tonight he would talk with Miss Alford, confess his own feelings, and ask for her help and advice. There must be some way out of this agonizing dilemma!

Chapter Nine

There was to be one more interruption in the even tenor of the day's activities. Late that afternoon, when the kitchen maids (still inclined to giggle as they reminded one another of the defeat of the attack upon the castle, and the routing of merchant Wallace) were preparing a special evening meal for the augmented staff, word came that a message had been delivered from the village by young Colin Wallace.

"Bring the boy into the kitchen for a glass of ale," ordered Fredricks. "I can't disturb the major now." While they waited to welcome young Colin, Polly spoke out.

"What's the ol' man about now?" fretted the girl. "Will we have to put up with him stickin' his nose in all the time, jus' because his son's our new factor?"

Matilda gave her old friend a knowing glance, but her tone was casual as she asked, "Do you think Ian Wallace will make a good factor for the major, Polly?"

The girl fell easily into the gentle trap. Her small face lighted from within. "Oh, milady, I'm sure he'll be a great success! He's very bright; you heard the minister say that! And he's—he's resolute, and loyal—" Her breath failed her, but she smiled widely.

"You do not feel his war injury will hold him back?" Matilda probed for the response she expected.

Polly was almost sputtering in her eagerness to refute the possibility. "*Nothing* would hold Ian Wallace back from his duty," she averred stoutly. "He's just like the major! *He's* injured in the war, too, and nothin' holds *him* back!"

Then the girl caught the delighted smile on Matilda's face, and her eyes widened. "Oh, Milady! You've been teasin' me, haven't you?"

"Let's just say I wanted to know how you felt about our new factor," Matilda said. "I think he's splendid, too!"

Shaking her curly head at the underhanded methods of the aristocracy, Polly returned to her task of carrying heaping trays of food to the table. A few minutes later the servants began to assemble in the huge kitchen for the meal, accompanied by young Colin. While everyone welcomed the boy, Miss Alford related to Matilda with keen interest that the butler, the sergeant, the new factor, and the laird, in solemn conference, had decided that the great drawbridge should be raised every night just after sunset. Since this usually occurred about nine-thirty at this time of year in this area, they had had all afternoon to work upon the ancient machinery.

"Such a delightful pastime for them," murmured the governess. "You will find, my dear child, that most men are like boys when presented with the opportunity to fiddle with anything mechanical."

Surprisingly the drawbridge mechanism, built by a former blacksmith of great local renown, had proved to be still as sound as a nut and was quickly placed in good working order with the application of suitable grease, both fat and elbow. The whole male staff seemed to feel they had gone a long way toward defending the laird's home with this labor. Fredricks privately told Matilda and Miss Alford that a hearty cheer had risen spontaneously as the great old bridge rose slowly up to the wall.

This general spirit of congratulation was maintained throughout the excellent meal. The new factor even ventured a mild joke about having to check the accounts if such a lavish spread was to be served every night.

"Well, Major, I *tried*!" he said mock-solemnly.

Matilda watched her major as he deftly guided his new clan in their friendly discovery and acceptance of one another. He is wonderful, she thought, with a wistful sigh. How can I hope to be a fitting wife for such a man? He is right to have second thoughts about marrying me! She had convinced herself, during the long day, that she must say nothing to anyone, not even dear Alford, about her problem. The laird would have to make his own decisions, in his own time.

Meanwhile the major, who had finally had a moment to talk with his youngest guest, had invited the messenger to remain overnight in the castle, if he thought his mother would not be worried.

"Oh, my mother expects it," the boy said blithely. "She even sent along a clean shirt with me, and I'm to sleep in Ian's room, so as not to put anyone out."

Smothering a smile—for he had wanted to be accepted as the laird, had he not? and being the laird evidently meant being responsible for all the neighborhood—Robert Bruce went off to his own suite of rooms in the North Tower. He had intended leaving the renovating of his own quarters till last, but the enthusiasm of his servants had compelled him to permit them to furbish up the laird's rooms. Now he found the huge bedroom, the gracious sitting room, even the little cubby of a bathroom set out from the wall above the moat, to be a comfort and a place of restoration.

"I could come to love this old wreck of a castle," the major grumbled, sinking into the laird's chair, an enormous padded armchair he'd bought in Edinburgh, with a groan of relief. He would never show weariness before his staff, but there were times, like tonight, when his very bones seemed to ache. "I am an old man," he thought, "too old for my lovely girl. . . . "

But he could not let such despairing thoughts weaken him. There was the letter Colin had brought. The major opened it. With a growing frown, he perused the written lines.

No! Quickly he turned to the signature. He'd never heard of the fellow. The message read:

Dear Major Bruce:
It has come to my attention that my great-uncle, Willum Bruce, has died, and that a search for heirs has been instituted. I know you will be delighted to hear that I am the closest in line to Laird Bruce. I have been on the Continent with my sister, which is why the lawyers were not able to find me sooner. I know you will be glad to have the wretched business of settling up the debts and arranging family affairs taken off your hands. I am setting out from Edinburgh immediately after I post this missive, and will be with you to take over at Glenholme soon after this reaches you.

Your cousin,
Hubert Bruce-Talon

The devil you will! raged Major Robert Bruce. For he had realized, in that shocking moment, that he loved the old wreck of a castle with a fiercely possessive love, and would defend his right to it through rack and ruin—to the death!

Chapter Ten

Immediately after breakfast the following morning, the major called a Council-of-War. Everyone, from Fredricks to young Colin, was commanded to attend him in the Great Hall. An alarming note was struck when the major told McLeod not to lower the drawbridge until after the meeting—"for we are, in effect, under siege."

There was a shocked silence, out of which came a wail from young Colin. "Not my Dad again?"

No one laughed. Every eye, anxiously seeking information, was trained upon the dark, set face of the master of Glenholme. For he was the master—the laird. Even the women servants could read the force of Robert Bruce's iron determination in his stern countenance. This was not the man who had joked with them, given sly digs at the encroaching merchant, eaten at their table with them. Oh, the camaraderie was still there, but now it was buried under a grim and purposeful arrogance. The laird's first words confirmed the truth of this.

"I wish you to share with me a piece of news that I received last night. As members of my clan—my true liege men and women—it is your right to know when our home is threatened . . . when our right to serve Glenholme is challenged. . . . "

The laird paused, staring around, meeting every eye. His audience hardly dared to draw a breath lest they miss a word of explanation about the threat. After a brief pause, the laird spoke again.

"I suppose I should first ask you if I have presumed too much. Are you my liege men? Is it your free will to join the clan Bruce; to swear allegiance to me as its leader and laird? I would not coerce any one of you. If you do not wish to remain here, if you do not wish to take part in the coming struggle, you have only to speak now. Be assured I shall pay your wages and give you handsel to keep you until you find another place—"

Ian Wallace's voice rang out loud and clear in the stunned silence. "What threatens us at Castle Glenholme, Laird? We must know, if we are to be of help to you."

There was a rising murmur of agreement, and then Matilda's firm tones rose above it. "You know we are with you *à outrance*, Laird Bruce," she said.

For the first time since he had read the shocking letter the night before, Robert Bruce smiled. "And so say all of you?" he challenged. " *'The will to do; the soul to dare'?*"

The chorus of assent rang loud.

The laird held up his hand in a gesture of triumph. Then he pulled the letter from his jacket pocket and read it out clearly, so everyone in the Great Hall could hear every word. When he finished, there was another silence. The clan seemed to be waiting for Bruce to speak. After a moment, he said, with the air of one picking up a gauntlet thrown down in challenge, "*So be it!* The gentleman informs me he is the true leader of our sept of the clan, the true heir of Lord Willum. Yet the men-at-law who sought me out with the news of my inheritance, who had me brought back from the hospital in Spain where I was recuperating from my wound, made no mention of another claimant. In fact, they assured me I was the only known descendant of Willum Robert Bruce, that all the other members of our particular branch of the family were dead. So it seems we must now decide what we are to do about this Hubert Bruce-Talon."

"You must write at once to the men-at-law in London and inform them of this new claimant," said Miss Alford.

"You had better retain a barrister in Edinburgh to give you quicker help," suggested Fredricks. "Letters to London take time, and if we are to go by that screed, we haven't any time to waste."

"I say we keep the drawbridge up, purchase guns and bullets, and sharpen our swords," said McLeod shortly.

Surprisingly there was a general cheer from the menservants.

The laird grinned widely. Matilda was relieved to see that the hard, drawn look had faded from his face, to be replaced by an almost boyish pleasure. It did his heart good to hear our united response to his problem, she told herself happily. He is a splendid leader, but he does not seem to realize how much loyalty he has won in this brief time.

"First," began the laird in a much brighter voice, "we must find out whether anyone in the valley has heard of the pretender. Have any of *you* ever heard of a Hubert Bruce-Talon?"

It seemed that no one had. "I'll ask the Reverend Cameron when I'm in the village collecting guns and bullets," piped up Colin Wallace eagerly.

His brother joined the general laughter but said to Major Bruce, "The boy may have a notion there, laird. Two notions. George Cameron would know, if anybody would. And we probably ought to lay in a few weapons, just in case."

The laird studied his factor's expression. "I believe you are hungry for action, Ian," he commented. "But you are right. We may need all the information and other support we can get before we're through here. And while you are in the village, I have some errands for you. First, ask your mother if Colin may act as an intelligencer for us. He can find out what the new man has to say to the villagers.''

"Good idea," agreed the factor. "He'll do it." One look at the boy's face was enough to convince them all that there was nothing the young lad would like better than to play the spy against the pretender.

Matilda had been thinking hard. "Do you intend to deny him a room here in the castle?" she asked.

Everyone stared at her. There were a few frowns. The laird said slowly, "Do you think we should open the gates to one who wishes to dispossess us?"

"I think that an impostor—which I am sure from his letter he is—is better kept here under your eye, than running loose in the village, or worse, getting himself sponsored by some of the neighborhood bigwigs. If he is under your eye, you can surely prevent him from doing you too much harm." She looked pleadingly at her enigmatic soldier, who had just recently asked her to marry him. With a sense of relief, she understood that he might not have wished to discuss so personal a matter while he was facing such a frightening challenge. She longed to assure him that she would marry him if he had only the clothes he stood up in; that she would gladly walk the roads with him, or work in an inn kitchen for him, if he cared to share his life with her. But, of course, she could not say any such thing in this council meeting. So Matilda tried to put it all into the glance she gave him.

Whether or not she was successful, she did not know, but her major gave her his wide, warm smile.

"I think Lady Matilda has a good point, do you not?" he addressed the group. "Perhaps it would be wiser to keep the pretender under our close scrutiny. I shall count on you all to treat—*our guest*—with courtesy, but you don't have to cater to his whims and foibles," he ended, with a look that set them all to chuckling.

"Now, unless anyone has a suggestion to make, we had

better get our plans into action. Jem,'' addressing one of the grooms he had hired in London, "I'd like you to take a letter to London to the lawyers. Ian will see you have money for the trip, and you may take a good horse. I'd like you to get there as quickly as possible.''

"Right, sir.'' Jem stood up, happy to have an important task to do. "Shall I get ready right away, sir?''

"Please. I'll have the note ready by the time you are. You will wait for their answer. Plan to stay at least two nights in London. Come to me here when you're ready to ride.''

When Jem had left the Hall, the laird addressed the rest of his staff. "Any ideas?''

"There really is something havey-cavey about that letter,'' Matilda spoke slowly. "As you said, if this man was an heir, why didn't the lawyers mention him? Oh, I know he says he's been on the Continent, but you were on the Continent, too, in some obscure Spanish hostel, and they found you. But it's more than that. He seems to want you out *very quickly*. He's not willing to wait for due process of law. I think he is trying to push you out or scare you away before you have time to investigate his claim. Whatever he says or does, I would not leave this castle—if I were you,'' she added in a smaller voice. I hope he will not consider me presumptuous! she thought.

The laird did not seem to think any such thing. He gave her his wide smile. "You are reminding us that *possession* is nine points of the law,'' he answered. "I believe you are right. Our pretender does seem very anxious to 'take over,' as he said in his letter. Let us keep him under surveillance for a while till we discover just what he's up to. Are we all agreed on that?''

There was not a single dissenting voice. The laird then thanked them for their advice and loyalty and formally closed the Council. The liege men and women, feeling very important because the laird had shared his problem with them—and not seeing anything odd in the fact that London-born servants should suddenly find themselves part of a Scottish clan—went eagerly back to their tasks, quietly discussing the pretender and their roles in the defense of Glenholme.

When only Matilda, Miss Alford, Fredricks, and McLeod were left in the Great Hall, Major Bruce regarded them with one dark eyebrow raised quizzically. "I seem to have landed all of you in a questionable situation," he said.

The eager partisanship of their replies must have warmed his heart, for he smiled at them as he continued ruefully, "I thank you, my special friends, but we have to consider that the pretender may be very much more to the liking of the villagers and the local gentry than ever Major Bruce was. You all know that not a single one of my neighbors has come to call upon me, which they should in all courtesy have done had they been willing to accept me as laird of Glenholme. They may all be glad to see the Sassenach put in his place—outside the walls."

Matilda said stoutly, "You won over the villagers—at least every one who came to see you. And now that you have hired so many of them to work here, at a good salary, they will be most reluctant to see you thrust out."

"That makes good sense, sir," agreed Fredricks. "Perhaps this pretender's threat is what you need to win over the nobs, just as you did the villagers."

But the major was not sure. "Maybe this Hubert Bruce-Talon will be more to their liking than a mere major, and a crippled one at that. Some of them may even know him."

There was a glum silence as they digested this unpalatable idea.

Then Matilda said, "Why don't we ask them all to dinner and give them their chance to decide?"

While the other three looked at the girl in shocked surprise, the major grinned. "You are so sure they will prefer me to the pretender?" he asked gently. "So much trust is—heartwarming.'' But somehow everyone realized that the opposite reaction was even more likely to occur among the hidebound old families in the district. Matilda had a horrifying vision of the Great Hall furbished for a reception—and no guests! It would be a hard hurt to live down.

"I—I hadn't thought that anyone might refuse the laird . . . '' she faltered, her eyes seeking the major's weather-tanned countenance. It was the focus of four pairs of eyes; in fact, all concerned for his dignity and his pride.

In return, the laird fixed his loyal adherents with a gaze that had all the arrogance of a bared broadsword. He nodded once, sharply.

"I have made my decision,'' he told them, hard-voiced. "No Bruce has ever avoided a challenge! All that remains is for you four to back me up. Will you agree to be guided by me in this matter?''

"Oh, yes!'' breathed Matilda, her great eyes adoring the big soldier. Her admiration was so evident that the other four found themselves smiling in sympathy. Catching this reaction, the girl strove to conceal her love. Miss Alford moved to protect her too-vulnerable charge.

"It might help us to give you the assistance you desire if we knew what was this matter to which you refer,'' she said crisply.

Color darkened the major's cheeks, but his gray eyes held steady. "I intend to marry Lady Matilda Mountavon, at once, at Gretna Green, and then return with her to Castle Glenholme, where we shall have a celebration that will include the whole neighborhood—the whole county! And be damned to them if they don't come!''

Now four stunned countenances were turned to his. Unable to credit what they had just heard, they stammered, murmured, babbled, until one clear voice rose above the jangle.

"I'll come!" vowed Matilda devoutly. "That is, I accept!''

There was a chuckle from the men as she moved toward her major, with the obvious intention of casting herself upon his manly bosom. Gone were her doubts, reservations—if she had ever had any. This was no moment for poor-spiritedness!

The major received her in his one arm, but it was the laird who pressed a chaste kiss on her brow, held her close for a moment, and then smiled grimly at their audience.

"You are aware of the problems we face," he told them. "It shall be the duty of all of us to protect my Merielle from even a breath of calumny."

Even Miss Alford nodded grimly at this. Perhaps more than either Fredricks or McLeod, the governess knew the frightful perils that beset the plan. Social ruin, a lifetime of rejection and scorn—and, if the pretender's claim proved valid, not even the comfort of the major's beloved castle would remain to them. But none of the loyal friends standing so supportively beside the major and his Merielle would have had it any other way. What a truly superb challenge!

Chapter Eleven

Only two persons accompanied the laird and his bride-to-be on the secret flight to the famous smithy at Gretna Green. Just within the border of Scotland, it had for decades been a place where runaway couples from England could be married without parental consent.

Matilda—looking, the major thought, adorable in a soft, ruffled white dress—was seated with Miss Alford, herself quite elegant in her finest costume. Facing them, the major and his faithful McLeod, immaculate in their newly furbished uniforms, had an excellent opportunity to observe the various emotions that passed across the expressive little countenance of the major's love. Chief among these was a keen interest in everything to do with their destination.

"Will we really just clasp hands over an old anvil?" she queried. "It seems . . . rather flat."

The major sternly repressed a laugh. "There is much more to it than that," he instructed her. "We are required to declare, in front of witnesses, that we wish to become husband and wife." His endearing grin could not be suppressed any longer, and he added, laughing eyes on her face, "I only hope my voice will not play me up! I should hate to wed you with a squeak!"

The two ladies stared at him in surprise. Then Matilda's

sweet smile blossomed in response to his little joke. She had never seen her big soldier so lighthearted, carefree! Did the prospect of marrying her really bring him so much joy? It was a heartening idea. Blushing a little, she asked, "Do we both say it? If we speak in unison, it won't be so obvious if one of us squeaks."

"A duet?" considered the major. "Should we sing? Or should we leave that to Miss Alford and McLeod?"

Even the sergeant was grinning now, and Miss Alford said, over a ripple of laughter, "I'll have you know, Major Bruce, that I was accounted to have rather a fine soprano in my younger days. Better not tempt fate, or you may get a solo!"

In perfect accord, the foursome reached Gretna and at once sought out the smithy.

"Please forgive me for rushing matters, my darling," the major breathed into his Merielle's small ear. "When you are safely mine, we shall have time for refreshment and comfort, but now—!"

Since there was indeed a wary, anxious gleam in the silver eyes, Matilda made no objections to the hurried ceremony.

In the event, the major's voice rang out clear and strong, and Matilda's, while soft, was firm. Miss Alford, in spite of having warned herself not to become sentimental, was forced to wipe away a few tears. McLeod wrung his master's hand with great fervency and quite amazed them all by bending his head above the bride's hand with gallant panache.

Glenholme's new mistress looked at her laird with eyes gleaming with happiness. "I love you," she breathed, for his ears alone.

Her husband placed his arm around her with infinite gentleness. "As I do you," he acknowledged softly. "Until death—and beyond."

Even the Scottish participants, accustomed to emotional scenes of many kinds in this place, were moved by the sweetness of the little bride and the ardent sincerity of her new groom.

The major made up for the haste and lack of ceremony of the wedding by the style and richness of the marriage feast in the finest of the local inns. From somewhere he had even managed to obtain a posy of fresh flowers for his bride. Matilda cried into them. Everyone was pleased at this display of a natural and proper emotion. It was all delightful, if a trifle maudlin.

And then they had to face the return to Glenholme, with the inevitable problems and threats of disaster. For some reason, Matilda was more apprehensive than her major, who seemed to have something else on his mind. After trying to get him to discuss his strategy with her, and getting only the vaguest of irrelevant answers, she finally gave up and settled against the side of his big chest, cuddled in the curve of his strong arm against the jolting of the carriage. And fell asleep. After all, it had been an exciting day.

Over the girl's head three pairs of eyes met. Smiles were exchanged, and a quiet joy was shared.

And then Miss Alford spoke. She began soberly, in a very low voice, so as not to disturb the sleeping girl.

"This may be the best time to introduce an important subject." Both men fixed their gaze on her solemn face. "The marriage," she continued. "Binding, yes. And rendered beautiful by the sincerity of the participants." She hesitated.

"But—?" prodded the major.

"There will be talk," the governess went on grimly. "And disapproval. The Reverend Cameron will lead the chorus."

Unaccountably the major grinned. "I think not," he said softly. "I have been studying the good man, remembering how he was unable to refuse me welcome when placed in the situation by the merchant. So, before we left—in fact, while you were dressing my dear wife in her bridal finery—I called upon the Reverend Cameron and told him about my dilemma. Oh, yes! the whole sordid tale of the gamester-parent, the vicious evildoer, and the wicked bargain." The major paused, ruminating. "Cameron is a sentimental romantic under that pompous facade. He was so moved by Matilda's plight, so incensed at the evil results of gambling, that he agreed to marry us at a good, solid Presbyterian ceremony as soon as we get back to Glenholme. He was even sure there were some family rings in the old miser Willum's strongbox. I authorized Ian to help him find one."

The governess and the sergeant were staring openmouthed at this Machiavellian maneuver. The major chuckled.

"Do you think I would expose our darling girl to gossip? In fact, if there is any chance that she might find herself ostracized upon my account, I shall remove her, and all of us, to some more hospitable clime. The south of England, perhaps," he mused. "I saw some truly beautiful old homes there as McLeod and I drove up to London."

McLeod stared at him hard. "You would remove the whole staff of us? Bring everyone to your new home?"

The major lifted an eyebrow. "Of course. They have proved loyal and eager to work. I should not think of abandoning them."

"Even the ones who live in Glenholme village?" prodded the sergeant.

The major frowned. "I had not thought of that! I somehow considered them all as part of my household—"

"Spoken like a true laird," teased Matilda, who, awakened by the conversation, had listened to it with enjoyment. "It is no wonder they have loyalty for you, your lairdship—" she chuckled.

"If you call me that, Wife, I shall be tempted to beat you," growled her husband, giving her a firm hug before removing his arm with a slight wince, which did not, however, escape McLeod's notice.

"Does your arm pain you, sir?" he demanded.

The major stretched it. "No. Just a little stiff from its long duty-watch." The men shared a grin, as Matilda sniffed repressively, and Miss Alford made no effort to conceal a fatuous smile. Really, the man was devastating: handsome, upstanding, charming, intelligent, and every inch a man of high principles and integrity. Matilda was the luckiest girl in nature! When Miss Alford considered the alternative: the lecherous Tark; the cruel, unloving parents; even the possibility of a life as a servant in some grubby inn, she could only thank God that the major had been able and willing to rescue her darling. Miss Alford was as besotted with the major as Matilda was.

When they finally reached Castle Glenholme, they found that the Reverend Cameron had not been idle. As good as his word—or even better, thought the major with satisfaction—he had rallied the servants, the villagers, and even, wonder of wonders! had managed to dragoon the most devout of the local gentry! With who knew what appeals to Christian charity or threats of eternal perdition, grinned the soldier. The castle itself was a feast of lights: flambeaux and torches bloomed from every prominence. The drawbridge was down; the gates were open; flowers, including heather, adorned the Great Hall, where the servants were ranged in their best attire. The major and his party stopped at the entrance to the Hall, and for once in his well-controlled life, the major was at a loss for words.

His face said it all. Led unobtrusively by Fredricks, who recognized his moment, the staff broke into cheers. Cries of "Long live the laird!" and *"Bruce! Bruce!"* rang in the enormous vault and echoed from the beams high above. The Reverend Cameron was not far behind in leading the gentry in welcome. He trod the way toward the major's party, now following their laird into the Great Hall. Miss Alford quickly herded her charges into a receiving line, headed by the laird, then his wife, then Ian Wallace, the laird's factor. It was a meager line, but it would have to do, she fretted, watching Fredricks rally the servants into distributing trays full of drink for toasting the occasion and McLeod vanishing back toward the drawbridge and his patrol. She herself took up a position behind Matilda, although not in the line. And the Reverend Cameron, she was pleased to note, had taken *his* correct place at the major's other shoulder, where he was in position to introduce the guests as they came to the line.

Miss Alford nodded her satisfaction. All was proceeding with due formality—not even a high stickler could object to a single feature of the performance or the setting! And her dear Matilda had been carefully drilled to take her proper role in any formal gathering. Beaming, she observed the slight, girlish figure from the back.

Matilda was so concerned that no one should find anything to the major's disparagement that she quite forgot her own importance in this social exercise. For that reason, she gave the appearance of complete and correct self-possession, modest yet confident, such as must please even the most fastidious of persons. Her rather plain small face, whose only beautiful feature were the large dark-gold eyes, seemed lighted from within by a subtle radiance one could only call love. And each time her husband turned to make her aware of a new personage, her soft, rosy mouth broke into a smile that was very appealing.

The wife of the MacDonnell, who had had reservations about her husband's excess of Christian charity in welcoming an English upstart, found herself melting under the dazzling warmth of a white smile in a dark soldier's face. She then succumbed completely to the open innocence in the child-bride's countenance. This was no toplofty Sassenach, no wily female, but a well-behaved child obviously devoted to her tall, gallant groom. Lady Margaret at once forgave her spouse and the Reverend Cameron, who had required her presence here to celebrate the marriage. Glancing back for her husband, Margaret MacDonnell saw him clasping the one hand of the new laird, without embarrassment. The older woman smiled. Her husband, while no noddy, was not a particularly sensitive man. Still, he accepted that one brown hand with no indication in his manner that he was carefully favoring a crippled man. She looked again at the laird of Glenholme. Without knowing it, she chose the very word Miss Alford had selected earlier: *integrity*. It meant complete, whole, as well as upright, honest, and sincere. This new laird was a very different proposition from old Willum. Even with one arm, he was a very complete man!

This, indeed, seemed to be the opinion of most of the guests as they allowed themselves to be marshalled onto chairs to witness the wedding ceremony. They all seemed relieved that they had not been brought on a wild-goose chase by the Reverend Cameron. Their doubts and objections had been lessened by the evident breeding and impeccable courtesy of their host and his bride. And possibly also, a little, by the generous potations being offered by the servants. Before there could be time for second thoughts or a more stringent analysis of the situation, the Reverend Cameron had summoned them to witness the wedding of Robert Bruce, laird of Glenholme, and Lady Matilda Mountavon, spinster, of the parish of London.

Chapter Twelve

So they were married, the major and his Merielle.

After the brief ceremony, the guests gathered around the laird's table and enjoyed the elegant and satisfying repast that Fredricks and Polly had planned. Matilda, sampling the delicious food, was proud of her loving servants, who had worked so hard and so well to do her honor. Glancing around the table, she could see that all the guests were relishing the viands and especially the liquors they were plied with by the cheerful servants.

Lady Margaret, seated on the other side of the laird, leaned over to address the bride. "Your husband is to be congratulated," she said pleasantly. "I have seldom enjoyed such gracious hospitality, and never before at Castle Glenholme."

"I think the castle itself enjoys having its new laird," Matilda said romantically. "It truly welcomed us as we came in tonight."

Lady Margaret was willing to forgive such sentimentality in a new bride. "This happy occasion does seem to signal the beginning of a new and brighter period for Glenholme," her ladyship admitted. "That horrid old creature Willum Bruce offended every person in the county. You will find many who refuse to acknowledge you," she warned.

Her husband leaned his heavy, ponderous body forward to engage in the conversation. "Took a scunner to the auld miser, all of us did," he confirmed his wife's comment. "The auld limmer seemed to take pleasure in putting folks' backs up."

"I should venture to say that he was universally hated," the Reverend Cameron confirmed soberly. He sighed.

Lady Margaret said crisply, "He made the name of Bruce anathema in the county."

"In Scotland? I cannot accept that!" teased the major with a laugh.

Both the MacDonnells smiled reluctantly. "Well, at least he diminished this sept of the clan," said Lady Margaret.

"Do not tell me that I, innocent of his crimes, must pay for the old rascal's sins, milady," coaxed the major, with his charming smile white in the weather-darkened face. "After all, I never even met the man!"

This was brought out with such a boyish air of protest that even the dourest of his visitors were forced to chuckle. It seemed that the new laird was in a fair way to wiping out the transgressions of his predecessor.

Fredricks signaled the menservants to refill the guests' glasses and himself presented the delicious bride's cakes the maids had prepared. The evening became a huge success, so much so that the laird, ever mindful of his reputation in the district, sent outriders with every carriageful of guests, to make sure they found their way home without injury. Even the temperate cleric was happy to have a guide.

When the last guest had rather reluctantly departed, the laird called his servants to him. "I must thank you, one and all, for this superb celebration of my marriage. I should like to give you all a holiday tomorrow, but I am reminded that the pretender may arrive at our gates, and I need your support." His smile took in every member of the group. "So we shall have to man our battlements, I am afraid, but let there be no special housekeeping efforts made. Just a resampling of these tasty goodies with which you have supplied us so generously and the merest dust and polish of the Great Hall and the room the claimant will have."

He interrupted himself with a disarming grin. "I seem to be setting up a regular duty roster! So much for my idle words about a much-deserved holiday! I promise you, you will not go unrewarded, whatever happens. Thank you, and good night!"

He offered his arm to Matilda with a loving, supportive gesture, and the girl took it gladly. She was dazed with weariness, love, and a certain suppressed excitement. No one, not even Miss Alford, had fully explained to her the intricacies of the ritual that she would be sharing with her dear laird in a few minutes. Rather anxiously she peered up into his beloved dark face.

He looked very tired. It had been a long and demanding day and an exhausting evening. Her laird had carried it off gallantly, but she knew it had not been easy, and her heart swelled with concern and love.

"Soon you will be resting in your bed, dear Robert," she whispered, not wanting any ears but his to hear her. "I shall do all I can to ease and comfort you!"

She had apparently said the right thing. Her husband's face at once took on a brightness, an expression of alert happiness and expectancy. He stared down into the small, weary face, then gave her a tender glance as he guided her into the North Tower and thence to his rooms. The girl hardly realized where they were going until he closed the huge door gently behind them. Then she roused herself enough to stare around.

"Oh, this is very nice," she sighed. Hendricks had indeed outdone himself. There was a good fire in the great fireplace; the room was fragrant with the scents of heather and lavender. On the massive four-poster, the hangings were fresh and the covers crisp and clean.

The laird led his little bride to the bed. When she halted beside it, she looked up into his strong features with trust and loving expectation.

"You will have to instruct me, dear Robert . . . *Bruce*." She smiled.

The man caught her slight form to his chest with a hard arm. Smiling down into her uplifted face, he said, "I see you have learned your first lesson well, dear wife," and put his lips softly against the enchanting pout. Matilda melted against his hard body with utter satisfaction.

Her husband watched the contented little face with tenderness. Then he undressed her deftly, with reverence and consideration. As he proceeded, Matilda's eyes opened drowsily. She observed her condition, frowned, glanced quickly up at the major, and then relaxed again.

The major set his jaw. She was so adorable, so enticing—so trusting! He only hoped he had enough control to make this night the beautiful experience he wanted for her. Did she really know nothing? Was the little whispered offer in the Great Hall merely a comforting gesture because of his own tiredness? He hugged her for a moment, not trying to continue his task of undressing her or to speak to her. The great golden eyes were hidden under heavy lids; the rosy mouth was softly pouted as it was when she said his name. Squaring his shoulders, the major accepted his fate.

"My dearest girl, do you think you can rouse yourself enough to wash, and don your nightgear? I believe Miss Alford has had it placed on the bed."

Matilda blinked, looked up at him, and stifled a yawn.

The laird grinned. "Get into bed, you little wretch!" he said lovingly. "I'll wash myself and come to you shortly. And then I think there are some things I must explain to you—my very dearest wife."

But when he came back to her ten minutes later, Matilda was fast asleep. The major stood looking down at her for a long time, his eyes infinitely tender. Then, sighing, he got into bed beside her quietly and fell asleep with his arm around her.

Chapter Thirteen

The following day everyone in the castle was prepared to repel invaders—and nothing happened. When evening came and the drawbridge was raised safely for the night, the laird told his retainers, who had been waiting as tensely as he for the descent of the pretender, that they must all be thankful for the time of grace. Later, however, he confided to his little love that he would welcome the arrival of Hubert Bruce-Talon.

"Just to get the business over with," he confessed wryly. "Before the battle begins is always the worst time. When the lines are drawn and one's strength committed, then idle fears and fancies are easily forgotten in the excitement of action."

"Waiting is hard," agreed Matilda in a very small voice.

Her big husband scanned the small, forlorn face with dawning understanding. "It has been a dreadfully flat wedding-after day for you, my dearest, has it not?" he commiserated softly, taking her into his arms and leading her to his big chair before the fire. "Come here, wife, and let me love you!"

Matilda sank onto his lap with a sigh of relief. "It has been a bit lonely," she admitted. "Miss Alford and I realized that nothing in the way of—of a honeymoon could be considered as long as this threat hangs above us all. You cannot wish any harder than I do that the creature Hubert will come *and go* quickly!''

Although he knew how serious the matter was and had no wish to treat it lightly, the major was forced to smile at his love's obvious impatience. You failed to make her your own last night, he reminded himself. This wretched fellow threatens your happiness. Secure your territory tonight, lest the battle be joined tomorrow and another day be lost! He tightened his arm around the soft, fragrant little figure on his lap and hugged her close.

First placing a hard kiss upon the rosy lips—to state his claim—the major said quietly, ''You say you and Miss Alford discussed the honeymoon today?''

The great soft, golden eyes looked up at him. ''She asked me some questions that I did not understand exactly. They had to do with my comfort . . . '' She broke off, disconcerted by the intent gaze of her big soldier.

''I know what she was referring to,'' he said gently. ''I am only sorry that I had not been before her in instructing you— that is, in *showing* you—how much your love means to me.'' This is deuced awkward, the soldier thought, but it has to be done. Oh, my dearest little love, I want it to be perfect for you!

Gripping his courage firmly, he refreshed himself with one more kiss and began, ''When a man and woman are married—when they love each other as we do, they wish to share each other in every possible way.''

''Mmmm!'' agreed the girl blissfully, reaching up to taste his hard lips.

The major took a deep breath. ''One of the things they share is the joy of their bodies. They lie down together and become one.'' The man could feel sweat beading his forehead. This was harder than facing the villagers and the pretender combined. This was harder than Waterloo! He took a deep breath and continued, meeting the wide, loving, innocent gaze. "They undress and go to bed together and make love!"

There! It was out. He stared anxiously down into the absorbed small face. "Do you understand, my dearest heart?"

Matilda nodded happily. "Just as we did last night," she agreed.

The major groaned deeply in his chest. "No, my dearest. Last night you were fast asleep when I came to you. You looked so small and weary and peaceful that I had not the heart to waken you."

Matilda considered this thoughtfully. Finally she nodded. "I see. There are things we must do when we are together sharing your lovely big bed. And last night you were sorry for me and did not rouse me to do them."

The major groaned again, this time less violently. She was not stupid, his little love, but how could she comprehend matters that no one had ever discussed with her?

His wife surprised him. "We are neither of us asleep now, dear Robert. And the pretender cannot enter our castle until we lower the drawbridge. I think it is time you taught me the things that will enable us to share our love fully." She gave him her wide, lovely smile and put her arms around the strong column of his neck.

"Dear Robert! I cannot wait! I insist you begin at once!"

Groaning once again, this time with delight, her gallant major began to teach his adoring recruit all the secrets he knew—and found that the wonder of them increased a thousandfold in the teaching.

It was as well for the laird that this most important campaign was so brilliantly successful, for he needed all his confidence and strength the following day. Just after noon a servant came running with the word that a traveling chaise had been sighted upon the road to the castle. Matilda, who had been inspecting the burnished and beautiful Great Hall with him, turned her anxious attention to his beloved person. He was wearing his finest kilt and the dress jacket, which set off his big torso so well. Sporran; knee stockings; the skean dhu showing above the stocking top, even the plaid neatly draped over his shoulder to conceal the missing arm—all was as it should be.

"You are beautiful, my love," breathed the girl. "You will win your battles, my Bruce!"

Bending to place a swift kiss upon her rosy lips, the soldier strode briskly out to the wide stone steps of the entrance. His men were in their places behind the wall. Only McLeod and Factor Wallace, immaculate in new kilts, stood at his back. As the drawbridge was lowered, the major said softly, "He cannot take from us what we will not surrender. 'The will to do; the soul to dare'! *We shall hold fast!*"

Their growls of agreement were in his ears as the chaise pulled in under the arch and up to the steps.

It was a mediocre vehicle, the major thought loftily. Four wheels, two horses. It had the look of a hired carriage. Then his eyes widened in surprise at the golden youth who opened the door and swung out onto the stones of the courtyard. He was slight and smiling and elegantly dressed—and the most beautiful man the major had ever seen. Wide blue eyes, gently curling golden hair: features whose flawless molding caught the eye and held it. If this was the pretender, he was a formidable adversary! Doffing a modish hat in a sweeping bow to the major, he called out,

"I am Hubert Bruce-Talon, at your service! You must be the major?"

The soldier walked slowly down to extend his hand to the claimant. The clasp was brief and, on the youth's part, weak. Quickly disengaging his hand, Hubert turned back to the chaise and held out his arms. From the dark interior emerged a woman as beautiful in her way as the man was in his.

"My sister, Désirée," Hubert said proudly. "She has

come to share my good fortune with me as I claim my inheritance!''

Matilda, hovering anxiously in the shadows just inside the Hall, stared with dismay at the modish pair standing in the sunlight. The woman was so beautiful! No ordinary female, not even a wife, could hope to compete with that much style and dazzling good looks. And the pretender was so young and handsome—and so sure of himself! ''Claim my inheritance,'' he had said—and laughed confidently. Matilda moved forward to hear how Robert would reply to that blatant claim.

The major was executing a formal bow.

''This is—a pleasant surprise,'' he was saying calmly, in his deep voice. ''I bid you welcome to Castle Glenholme. Sergeant McLeod, will you see that one of the men shows Mr. Talon's groom to the stables? Now, Miss Talon, Mr. Talon, you must come in and meet my Lady.''

Matilda had noted the quick frown that had moved like a shadow across the golden countenance of the pretender. But at the major's last words, the frown was replaced by a blank look. Shock? Matilda pressed closer, eyes straining.

''Your . . . lady?'' For the first time, the beautiful woman spoke. From those flawless lips issued a voice a trifle shrill, speaking in an accent much less elegant than her costume. ''Your *mother* is here?''

''My Lady wife,'' the Major corrected her gently. ''When I received your brother's letter, I had hoped you might arrive in time to attend our wedding.''

As he spoke, the big soldier preceded his uninvited guests into the Great Hall, and so missed the dagger-sharp glances they exchanged. Matilda, however, advancing to meet the Talons with as much aplomb as she could summon up, did catch the exchange and felt the first deep prickle of doubt. She had said that she considered the pretender a rogue, up to no good, but she had not actually accepted the reality and the ramifications of such a deception. In all her lonely, too-sheltered eighteen years, she had had nothing to do with the ploys and deceptions of the "polite world," and even less with true criminal behavior. Then, a few moments ago, the golden, boyish presence of the claimant had seemed to deny the possibility of double-dealing. But there was nothing innocent nor youthful about that hard, silent interchange, and in a sickening flash of fear, Matilda was forced to accept that the threat was real, not an interesting game. It appeared that in real life, criminals did not all come in recognizable guises. She should never have insisted that the major welcome these creatures into the castle, making them free of the very heart of the defenses that should have been erected against them! But there was no time for second thoughts or even for devising plans. She must leave all that to her major and hope that he had not been taken in by the boyish charm of the pretender or the blatant good looks of his sister. If she really was his sister! Matilda pettishly thought, angry at her own stupidity as much as at the tricks of the deceivers.

The major was introducing them to her, and she forced herself to greet them with at least a semblance of courtesy. "I bid you welcome to Castle Glenholme," she found herself saying pompously.

She was quickly made aware of the force arrayed against her. Désirée Talon—if that truly was her name!—made a stylish curtsy and smiled coldly into Matilda's face.

"Why, I thank you, milady. And hope to have the opportunity of returning your welcome later, after my brother has taken his rightful place here as the laird."

The men most directly involved in the undeclared battle seemed uncomfortable with this open declaration of hostilities, for each of them turned to his female adherent with a cautioning glance. The major placed his arm gently about his wife's shoulders and said with a tender smile, "Ever loyal!

Shall we ask Miss Alford to show our guests to the South Tower, my love? I am sure they will wish to refresh themselves after their journey.''

The pretender had taken Désirée's arm in one hand and was urging her in the direction indicated by the major.

''You show yourself a worthy guardian of my estates,'' he said smoothly. ''I had been told that the old building was a ruin, but I see you have worked wonders. I am grateful and will make suitable recompense—when things are settled.''

The major's grin reassured Matilda. ''Yes, there must be due recompense—when things are settled,'' he agreed softly.

As the Talons prepared to follow the imperturbable Miss Alford, Désirée favored the major with a long, sultry stare and a slow smile. Matilda felt a pang of panic deeper than the one that had oppressed her at her first sight of the interlopers. The major will handle them, she encouraged herself. Unless, he is seduced by that—creature! Her self-confidence, never strong as the unvalued, unloved daughter of Mountavon, was dangerously threatened by the delectable Désirée. What man could resist her? As her anxious eyes met the steady silver glow of her husband's, she denied her treacherous weakness and caught at his hand.

''I am sure they are thieves,'' she whispered urgently. ''And that woman wants you! I should never have urged you to bring them into the castle.''

The major considered this. Was there a . . . sparkle in his eyes? wondered Matilda. He said, ''Yes, there is something very double-faced about our visitors. Tricksy, as our Scots friends would say. But aren't they the handsome ones! Miss Désirée is enough to make a sailor blush, with that leer she gave me as she left us!'' He rolled his eyes ridiculously. ''I hope you are jealous, milady?''

Their shared laughter eased the sharp pain in the girl's breast. Her husband continued seriously, ''Still, her overblown beauty and Talon's air of boyish charm will exert an influence upon the diehard gentry who have refused to accept me. It'll give them a way out. We'd better ask the pretty Talons about their background.''

''Do you think they'll tell us the truth?'' Matilda frowned. ''I cannot believe it. They undoubtedly have some story ready to spread abroad that will completely establish them and discredit us.''

Her husband was smiling down into her small, concerned face. ''But that will give us something to work on—even if it is only to prove them liars,'' he murmured. ''Why are we wasting time in talk of the creatures? I have hardly had an opportunity to bid you good morning today, much less to tell you how much I love you, darling Mrs. Bruce.'' He kissed her sweetly. ''And how much I appreciate your loyalty and your wisdom.''

''Wisdom?'' the girl mocked herself. ''I shall be thankful if I have not ruined everything with my childish suggestions! Have you a plan to discredit them?'' She peered hopefully up into his darkly tanned visage.

The major favored her with the wide, white grin she found so devastating. ''A plan? Perhaps. Or maybe I should just permit them to bring about their own doom. What's that good old phrase? Hoist with their own petard?''

Matilda's heart sank. What sort of a strategy was that? To allow the wretched creatures to work their will without let or hindrance? But when she said as much to her major, he merely chuckled and told her he had important work for her to do.

Comforted, she demanded to know what it was.

The daft fellow merely grinned at her and murmured provocatively, ''Say my name!''

At her involuntary scowl of annoyance, he threw his head back in a shout of laughter and kissed her so hard she forgot all her worries for a few delirious moments.

Her big new husband scanned her love-drugged expression with approval. ''That's ma braw wee lassie!'' he drawled in a broad Scots burr. "Ye mun keep that same besotted look upon yer bonnie little phiz, an' I'll no compleen!" He kissed her once more, with a very proprietary air.

With horror, Matilda realized that her husband was *enjoying* this dangerous situation.

Chapter Fourteen

When Matilda realized that her darling feckless husband was treating the very real menace of the usurping Talons with such lightheartedness, she sent at once for Miss Alford. Luckily that good woman had just returned from establishing the pretenders in their luxurious suites of roomes. As she heard this report, Matilda's frown darkened.

"It irks me to see such persons fussed over," she grumbled. "The South Tower, forsooth! That's the place for the women of Glenholme!" She caught the expression on Miss Alford's face and continued hastily, "It will make so much work for the maids! I have no doubt it will take the full time of one of them to look after these creatures."

"As I see it, it will take at least two," Miss Alford surprised her. "Full-time. Spying," she concluded triumphantly. "And Fredricks assigned a valet for Hubert."

Matilda could only be amazed and delighted at this evidence of double-dealing on the part of her faithful governess and butler. "But will that be enough?" she wondered. "Just watching them? Surely they will not betray themselves in front of our own people?"

Miss Alford gave a very wicked smile. "Just think of all the times they'll be *out* of their rooms," she gloated. "Nuncheons, luncheons, teatime, dinners! To say nothing of tours around the countryside—the list is endless! A good maidservant can have every drawer and cabinet opened for inspection before the cat can lick its ear! To say nothing of every portmanteau.'' She came closer and lowered her voice. ''As a matter of fact, I already have my doubts about the Talons. Not at all the thing, their luggage. And her clothes, while beautiful and—*daring*—are not such as one would expect from the sister of a lord.'' She nodded portentously. ''No, Milady, even if we accept that they have made a hurried journey from the Continent, and even that they may not have been well off while living or traveling there, we are still faced with a wardrobe unsuitable for the sort of persons they claim to be.''

This partisan announcement depressed rather than encouraged Matilda. It was clear that Miss Alford was completely devoted to her mistress and her new master, but utter devotion often blinds one to hazards, the girl thought desperately. Miss Alford was forgetting that the Talons would be trying to consolidate themselves with the local gentry. And which of that group, already deeply prejudiced against the English upstart and observing the coaxing charm of the golden youth and the desirable Désirée, would note or even care that her wardrobe was scanty and of questionable quality? They'll be too busy looking at those eyes, and that painted mouth, and that lustrous golden hair, to notice anything else! Well, honesty compelled her to make a reluctant addition, her more than bounteous figure, too!

Matilda set her small jaw belligerently. There must be something she could do! While she tried to think what it could be, she must not neglect to appreciate the loyalty of her old friends. ''Thank you, Alfer,'' she used her childish form of her governess's name. ''I'm sure the major, with our help, will find a way out of this mess.'' But the light in her fine amber eyes was not confident but anxious.

At this same time, McLeod was reporting to the major.

"It's a job-carriage, sir, and a cheap one at that. The jarvey who handles the reins is a sullen clod, and I couldn't get much out of him, except he was hired on in London to bring the Talons up here, and a precious hard bargain they drove. He says he hasn't been paid yet."

"Good," said the major. "Then he may be amenable to reason," and he rubbed his thumb and two fingers together suggestively.

McLeod scowled. "He's afraid of them, it seems," he admitted. "I find it hard to ken, but that smarmy yellow-headed boy seems to have put the fear into the jarvey."

The major's eyebrows rose. "Another surprise! Our darling boy can frighten his hired coachman! I see I must study our pretender more carefully."

"You do that, sir," advised McLeod soberly. "He's got a lot at stake here. But then, *so do we*."

On the basis of that last word, the major clapped his faithful sergeant on the shoulder and strolled from the room. McLeod stared after the tall, well-set-up figure and shook his head. The major took serious matters too lightly. But then, McLeod would never forget the lighthearted smile with which the big soldier had leaned down from his saddle and scooped the sergeant out of the way of the charging French cavalryman, accepting on his own left arm the sabre-blow meant for McLeod's unwary head.

Dinner that night was splendidly formal. The servants had outdone themselves. Matilda watched the faces of the Talons carefully and was pleased to observe that although they tried not to show it, they were impressed. Fredricks kept the wines and stronger liquors flowing. The major seemed to be indulging as freely as Hubert Talon, but Matilda was aware that although Fredricks bent over his glass with the different bottles, he did not always allow much to flow into the crystal.

Matilda focused her scrutiny upon the gorgeous Désirée. If the woman had been attending a formal dinner at the Palace, she would not have dressed finer, was the girl's disgruntled thought. Suddenly her own wardrobe, so carefully chosen by Miss Alford in Edinburgh at the major's generous insistence, seemed very *ingénue* and colorless compared with the opulent richness and dramatic colors of Désirée's garments. How can he resist her? wondered a despondent Matilda, noticing the thrusting curves of the older woman's bosom, openly displayed by the low-cut gown. He is accustomed to straightforward dealing with men on a field of battle, not coping with the tricks of devious witches and playacting cheats. She ground her teeth in helpless fury. The pretender—the adversary—had all the appearance of a charming youth—golden, ingenuous, open. For the major to move harshly against such a vulnerable target would brand him a cruel brute in the eyes of the neighbors. How would her dearest major conduct this uneven contest? Matilda took an unaccustomed deep draught of the wine in her glass and choked over it. She looked up to meet the amused, understanding glance in those wonderful silver eyes.

The major had already revised his earlier plans and was committed to a new strategy. It had taken him even less time than it had Matilda to realize that the Talons presented a real threat of an unexpected nature. This would be no open conflict, fairly fought. It would probably not be allowed by the Talons to come to a decent legal battle in which even the winner might have to wait years for the decision and pay handsomely for it as well. No, the major did not believe that the Talons had a real legal claim. There was none of the triumphant citing of facts: dates, names, supporting details, which surely would already have been given if the claim were a legitimate one. No, Major Bruce thought, I have to deal here with a couple of very sharp swindlers, but they have weapons that can wound me—and my darling girl—in ways that may never heal. If, for example, they ever discovered the business at Gretna Green! Or found out that Matilda's parents had not sanctioned the marriage—were completely ignorant of it! While no one could get the marriage annulled, a determined enemy could certainly destroy the reputation and consequence of Robert Bruce in the county. There were too many important people who had still not accepted the upstart Englishman as the laird of Glenholme. Any charges or disclosures the Talons made would, no doubt, be eagerly welcomed and used by the local powers.

The major took a refreshing sip of his great-uncle Willum's best brandy. Fredricks had protected him all through dinner against overindulgence, which might weaken his resistance and cause him to make some stupid mistake, while at the same time the wily butler had plied the Talons with the most persuasive liquors in the castle cellars. To little obvious avail, the major decided. While the golden-haired pretender was a trifle red-faced, his speech was still clear and his eye as cold and wary as ever.

Major Bruce made his decision. It was not for a wary, knowledgeable soldier to advance fiercely, blindly, against an obviously weak boy. That was how Saxon Harold had lost his life and his kingdom to the conquering William of Normandy: running madly downhill after an apparently retreating force. No, Major Bruce would meet his antagonist on his own field. The major grimaced wryly at his own arrogance in thinking he might outcharm, "outvulnerable," the golden youth. Then he took a clear glance at the flushed boyish face. And was pleased to note a soft pouching beneath the wide blue eyes and some heavy lines pulling at the rosy mouth. *Rosy?* Dear lord, thought the major with unholy glee, the fellow's painted his face! So much for ingenuous youth!

It was as heartening a sight as the arrival of a relief battalion at the crux of a battle.

It was gradually discernible that the major had either had

too much to drink or that he was in the grip of another, less acceptable emotion. Even the servants noted his gallant attentiveness toward the delectable Désirée. Matilda, unwilling to believe and yet forced to accept the coming to life of her darkest fears, made a covert scrutiny of the woman's brother.

Hubert Talon, by now darkly flushed by the potations he had downed, appeared to be wholly delighted with his sister's success in enchanting the redoubtable soldier. He made a few unsubtle innuendos, which brought him a minatory glance from Désirée and a most usurping announcement from her that the ladies would now leave the table and that her brother had better come with her to their rooms, since he was obviously overtired from his journey.

The major was interested to note that Hubert, after one brief angry glance at Désirée, had risen as she suggested and made his rather stumbling good nights. Definitely a pair of rascals, decided the soldier, and the woman perhaps the stronger. At least he respects her judgment so far. Well, we shall have to see.

Matilda was not at all annoyed that the woman Désirée had usurped her right as hostess to give the signal for the ladies to rise. She was so thankful to have her susceptible major removed from the hideous spell of the seductress that she could hardly manage to reply to the good nights or wait until the pretenders had been escorted out of the Great Hall to their rooms by a servant with a lighted candle. When they were at last gone, she turned upon the major with scarcely concealed hurt.

"How could you cater to that woman?" she demanded. "You were practically kissing her with your eyes!"

Her major grinned disconcertingly. "Was I, then?" he teased. "A difficult trick, surely? Let us go up to our room and practice it, milady. And some other tricks I thought of during this very boring dinner."

His wife looked at him askance. Was he teasing, or drunk? She had never had occasion to observe the behavior of a drunken man and so had nothing to compare his actions and speech with. And yet, if he were intoxicated, it had scarcely changed his normal behavior. Perhaps he was one of those she had heard Polly speak of, who could *hold their liquor*.

She sighed deeply, unaware how revealing her small, anxious face was.

The major smiled down at her. "This is one of the times when I most deeply regret losing my arm," he whispered. "What I should *like* to do now is to sweep you up in a close—a very close—embrace and bear you up to my bed like a veritable Ajax! Instead of which I may have to ask for your assistance on the stairs."

Not knowing whether or not to believe her exasperating, playacting spouse, Matilda was still unable to ignore the laughing plea in those warm silver eyes. With a little groan, she placed her arm securely around his big torso and pulled him close to her. Then she impelled them both toward the stairs. He let her hold him all the way to their room, even forcing her to manipulate the two of them through the door and close it after them. When, flushed and concerned, she brought him to a halt beside the huge bed, she looked up into his face to judge his condition. The rogue was laughing!

Before she could burst into an angry tirade, he tipped her gently onto their bed and covered her with his body.

For some reason, Matilda failed to demand the explanations she had fully decided must be given to her that night.

Chapter Fifteen

Matilda awoke late the following morning, ready to resume whatever sort of dialogue the major desired to initiate. To her dismay, he was not beside her. She considered this, meanwhile stretching luxuriously. It was possible that he had merely gone to order that food be brought to their bedroom to break their fast. A delicious thought! Or, perchance, having acquired a sense of his lairdly duty during the night, he had gone to keep an unobtrusive eye upon the activities of his self-invited guests. This thought should have comforted her. Instead she found herself feeling resentful of his absence from her side, and wishing the pretenders in Jericho or some other suitably distant area.

With a sigh for her own folly, Matilda rose, bathed from the bowl on the ancient chest, and donned a fresh and charming gown. She brushed her hair until it shone, telling herself rather shrewishly that at least its undistinguished chestnut brown was natural and not the result of foreign dyes. As she descended to the smaller dining room, where family breakfast was usually served, Matilda marveled at her own powers of observation. She had not consciously decided that the woman's rather brassily shining hair was unnatural, yet the knowledge was there, the restult of female intuition, no doubt! Rather smugly she wondered how anyone could have been deceived, even for a moment.

Armed with righteous disapproval and ready for the fray, Matilda found it a matter of some disappointment to discover that her only opponent was the childish Hubert. He greeted her cheerfully enough, but then proceeded to lose his advantage by informing her, with odious satisfaction, that her husband had taken Désirée for a tour of the castle.

Matilda surprised herself by the venomous sweetness of her answer. "Should it not have been you, as the supposed heir of Willum, who should have been given the tour? Or is it actually your sister who is the heir? She seems to have you under her control."

Both Matilda and the pretender were momentarily shocked by this blatant evidence of ill will from those soft, rosy lips. Hubert recovered first. The girl felt a frisson of alarm at the glare of vicious anger that flashed briefly over those perfect features. Suddenly the girl revised her estimate of her tablemate. This was no boy, but a devious and angry man. Hard lines grooved down from the flawless nose to bracket the lips; the wide, guileless blue eyes were narrowed and hostile.

Well, she told herself, striving for a grip on her fear, I always knew he was a charlatan, impostor, thief. But I did not understand just what a clever actor he is. That open, beautiful face concealed vicious greed; the boyish charm concealed a scheming man. Her fleeting glimpse of his true nature brought back all her alarm and shook her confidence in the major's ultimate victory. This had become one of those heroic contests about which Miss Alford had read to her: Cyclops challenging Ulysses; Charybdis stealing from Hercules; Medusa, the female monster, paralyzing every hero who dared to face her! The frightened thoughts raced on. Bravely she stole another glance at the male monster, only to observe the boyish, charming smile that was his habitual mask.

"It would seem that you must have had a rather disturbed night, Mrs. Bruce." His insinuating leer probed at her pale countenance. "Does it worry you that your new husband is so powerfully attracted to my sister? You must not let jealousy overcome you! My dear Désirée is forever enchanting men with her beauty and wit! She really cannot help it!" He shook his golden head in humorous dismay. Then, with another sly grin, he said softly, "Much better for the safety of your marriage to get Mr. Bruce back to England *very quickly*. Then you will be able to keep your husband, at least."

From somewhere deep inside her, she drew enough courage to smile.

"Thank you for your advice, Mr. Talon . . . if that is really your name. My husband's lawyers are carefully researching your claim, although you and your encroaching sister have not actually made one worthy of the name, have you? No documents offered to validate your statements? I wonder just what sort of noddies you consider us to be? As for my marriage, I have no need to feel alarm. My husband is an honorable man." Her scornful glance said all that her words had not, concerning her opinion of Hubert Talon's integrity.

The major, who had returned from the tour during this impassioned speech and was standing unnoticed in the open doorway, was torn between admiration, love, and a desire to turn the little firebrand over his knee. Talk about a lioness defending her mate! To say nothing of throwing down battle gages! To say nothing of throwing the cat among the pigeons! He grinned at his metaphors, as badly jumbled as his emotions. The little idiot had precipitated matters, brought the conflict into the open prematurely, perhaps disastrously. Yet even in the midst of his annoyance at his Matilda's too-hasty speech, the major realized that the tactical error had been his. He should have shared his information and his strategy with his junior officers, to prevent just this kind of over-eager loyalty, which might wreck his whole plan of campaign.

Then, strolling into the room on the heels of Matilda's dramatic defense, he caught a glimpse of the fury that writhed across Talon's face, twisting his features momentarily into a vicious mask. It was such a flash as Matilda had seen and been frightened by. The major knew he must divert that fury toward himself at all costs. His love-valiant little wife could never hope to win over such an unprincipled antagonist.

He coughed gently.

"Having a lovely breakfast?" he queried mildly, and then almost lost his poise to a gust of ironic laughter at the look of shocked surprise that his inanity evoked on the antagonists' faces. Closing his lips firmly against such a self-betrayal, he strolled over to the table and bent to plant a firm kiss on Matilda's cheek before he took his own seat at the table. He used that gesture to mutter a dire *"Shut up!"* in the girl's ear.

As he sat down, he bestowed a benign, lairdly smile upon his silenced table companions. The ridiculous elements in the situation, as always, clearly perceived by the major's rather off-center view of life and his fellow man, made it hard for him to concentrate at first. Then his years of military and self-discipline served him.

"Your beautiful sister enjoyed our tour of the castle, I think," he began innocently enough.

The pretender was back in control of his own emotions. "I knew she would!" he smiled ingenuously. "I told her to be sure to pay special attention, since she will be the mistress of the castle very shortly." Then, before his audience could make a comment, he went on, "I have instructed the butler to send out invitations in my name to all the local bigwigs, to meet the new laird and bid farewell to the good soldier who has worked so hard to prepare my inheritance for me. I mentioned that they must rally round the Sassenach at this hour to ease his natural disappointment. We'll all give you a hearty send-off."

"That was neatly done," nodded the major. "Quick, too. Hit the enemy before he knows he's engaged. It would appear to deal with all your problems in one—ah—fell swoop." He grinned tauntingly. "I would congratulate you, sir, upon your—ah—skill, except that your Désirée has already informed me that *she* gave those exact orders to my butler. It seems that she is the force to be reckoned with in this battle." His patronizing smile was enough to scorch the skin on any antagonist, Matilda thought fearfully. Why was he rushing so recklessly into this encounter?

"We shall have to see which of the three of us is the stronger, shall we not?" hissed the pretender, his boyish charm quite erased by his anger. Then he made a stumbling recovery. "In any event, whichever of us gave the order, the invitations have already been sent!" And let us see how you get out of that, his sneer said.

The major grinned. "When Fredricks brings me word of your presumptuous message, which, being the well-trained and loyal servant that he is, he inevitably will do, I shall of course order him to carry out the plan," he shocked both his hearers by saying.

"You will—?" Talon was unable to prevent the astonished words.

"I will," mocked the major. "While you have been so busy, I have not been idle. After all, you did give me over a weeks notice of your intent to capture the castle. Rather poor tactics, my boy," the soldier went on with odious smugness. "Better warn your Désirée that a good general does not inform his enemy of his most telling moves in advance."

This was too much to be borne. "It was not Désirée who dictated that letter—it was I!"

"My compliments to the lady," the major quipped insultingly. "I shall give her credit for having a little common sense." He rose and offered his arm to Matilda. "I have missed you this morning, my dear," he said with such quiet sincerity that the girl's heart began to beat faster. "Let us go for a stroll."

Without a backward glance at the discomfited Hubert, the major led his wife from the room.

When they were safe from surveillance, Matilda breathed, "I am afraid."

"Where is my stouthearted clanswoman?" teased the major; but his voice was gentle. "My mighty battle-maid?"

"They terrify me—both Talons," the girl confessed. "She is so beautiful . . . and attractive. And he looks like a delightful boy, but he is not! I have never met two such ruthless persons. With such smiling faces and caressing manners— yet all *false*!"

The major said gravely, "They are rather a common sort. Oh, I grant you these are prime articles, very exclusive merchandise indeed! But they come from lowly stock. Pinchbeck. Petty criminals, scavengers. Dozens of them follow the armies like vultures feeding on carrion—the scraps and bits of plunder that always clutter the path death has taken." His face had darkened as he spoke, recalling bitter memories. "I would not have you ignorant of their menace. I have seen their kind—the lesser ones—prowling over a battlefield, robbing the dead."

"Robbing—?"' gasped Matilda.

"Yes. There are always profits to be made! A ring, a coin or two, even a gun or a sword. To say nothing of a fine coat, if it is not too badly—stained." The major stopped himself, glimpsing the stern and sorrowing expression on the girl's face. He changed the subject.

"Come to our bedroom. I need to warn you of my plan, so that you will not give anything away at your next encounter with the enemy." To erase that darkling look, he said, with light self-mockery, "It would seem I have yet much to learn about leadership, to wit: Do not leave your junior officers in ignorance of your plan of campaign.''

Matilda felt a warm glow spreading throughout her body. That her splendid soldier should consider her as one of his staff! That he should feel comfortable about sharing his plans with her! It was a great gift.

The soldier saw and understood the glow that brightened the small countenance. He gave her a brief, hard hug, and then said firmly, ''To business, wife! Any more of this philandering and we shall be caught, unprepared, by the enemy.''

Dazed with happiness, Matilda would gladly have agreed to anything at this moment. The soldier, wise in the ways of the world, correctly evaluated her unquestioning adoration, and while he valued it and could wish for nothing better than to revel in the sensual delight it offered, still, this was not the time for love. It was, alas, a time for war.

''I have come to believe with you, that the Talons are not brother and sister,'' he began, deciding not to offend his darling's ears with the report of midnight-flitting from room to room, which Fredricks's observant staff had noted. ''I believe them to be a pair of greedy thieves who have happened upon the news of the long and thorough search for an heir to Glenholme. It may be that they overheard, or even were approached by, one of the agents sent out by the lawyers to find the last of this branch of the family. The exact circumstances that gave them their lead we may never know. What we do know is that they have seized upon this ploy to win them an easy fortune and a respected place in society.''

''It is their very good luck,'' he continued somberly, ''that the auld laird was so unlikable a character. We, alas, as first in the field, were the recipients of all the ill will the old curmudgeon had built up during his ninety years. We, as first claimants, were chosen to pay for all old Willum's sins in the neighborhood. Human nature being what it is, this leaves a fairly clean sheet for the new pretenders. *They* may well be viewed by our neighbors as a just punishment upon *me*, who was brash enough to put forward a claim to the estate and title of the old, well-hated laird.''

To the girl, listening with painful attention to this summary, the future began to appear very dark.

''What is your plan?'' she ventured.

''I must meet them on their own ground,'' he explained. ''Play a delaying action. They haven't given me much time, but I've instructed my lawyers by post to investigate the possibility that there's a real heir named Hubert Bruce-Talon. When he arrived here and staked his public claim so quickly, Hubert hoped to carry the day with arrogance and charm—to bluff the new heir. If that failed, Hubert could marry off the soldier to the beautiful Désirée.''

''But they found you already married,'' added Matilda with deep satisfaction. The major grinned.

''Since I was found to be impervious to the lady's wiles,'' he said primly, ''they probably decided to bullock the simpleminded soldier, who was, no doubt, used to taking orders from his superior officers. I'm sure they thought that was the real reason for my doltish reluctance to hand over the castle to them on demand. It probably seemed logical to Hubert to bring in the 'superior officers' in the persons of the powerful families in the district, most of whom had already refused to acknowledge me. Hubert must believe that once these men and women meet and approve of the beautiful claimants, the stubborn soldier will have to accept his dismissal. He'll become a straw dragon; completely harmless.'' The major frowned. ''I'm afraid I blurred that image a little by insisting upon sending out the invitations myself, but that can be easily attributed to my lack of the airs and graces of the haut ton. Who need fear a stubborn, doltish soldier who is also—most damning!—a cripple?''

Matilda reacted fiercely. "You are the most complete man I know!"

Her husband favored her with a softly teasing "But you don't know many men, do you, my darling?"

"They have misjudged our mettle!" insisted his little battle-maid.

The major awarded her his most devastating smile. "Indeed they have! I intend taking them at the point where, thinking they are strongest, they have set no guard. When they seek to disconcert the rough soldier and his child-bride with a showy display of elegance and specious charm, we shall be even more elegant and more charming. Thank God for Miss Alford," he said devoutly. "She has bred into you the niceties of deportment and social behavior that we shall need to convince our dour neighbors of our gentility. I shall have to play my part as the gallant, if slightly tongue-tied, soldier," he concluded with a wry smile.

Matilda's heart sank. Was that all the plan? To *behave better* than that wily, seductive pair of rascals? She must not let her darling realize how very flimsy and unpromising his scheme was! Perhaps the lawyers would have information that could save the day. Smiling determinedly, she said, "Of course we shall be our usual delightful, well-mannered selves. But what will we *do*?"

"While we are being delightful and well-mannered?" grinned her soldier. "You don't think that will do the trick, my love?"

With a heart overflowing with love for her too-credulous, naïf man, the girl took his big hand in both of hers and said earnestly, "What if those wretches have more than one plan for our downfall? The woman tried to seduce you without success. The man has not yet, thank God, tried to seduce me—" She caught a glimpse of a heavy frown drawing his black eyebrows together and hurried on. "—not that it would do him any good to try! But there is the invitation." In her

128

turn, she frowned at her husband. "You went along with that trick too easily, I fear! By agreeing to send it out, you have given them what they needed: well-wishers to encourage Hubert in his claim to the castle. You said yourself that most of the gentry do not acknowledge you!"

"The battle is scarcely engaged and already you mistrust my judgment?" asked her husband dramatically.

Matilda could not bear to meet those pleading silver eyes. "It is just that I am sure they have many reprehensible plans to destroy your claim to the title—and our peace," she whispered. Then she darted an anxious look up into the beloved face. . . .

The major was smiling! The wide white grin she adored.

"You find our problems—amusing?" she gasped.

"I am looking forward to their happy solution," admitted the soldier. "Tell me you trust me, my battle-maid!" he teased.

Matilda thought hard. She loved him so much! She must show confidence in his ability to rescue them from this danger. If he would only not be so lighthearted in the face of attack! But that was a good soldier's attitude, she reminded herself.

"With my life," she said simply. "But I fear the Talons."

"Then we must be on guard constantly, while being charming and well-mannered," he said. "I fear it is too much for a simple soldier." He heaved an ostentatious sigh, watching from the sides of his eyes how she was taking his raillery.

Matilda was of two minds whether to be angry or encouraged by the soldier's incorrigible joking. Perhaps it took that for him to keep up a strong front against his enemies? His playful attitude seemed ill-timed to her, when they should be bending every effort of mind and body to solve their urgent problems.

The major bent down and kissed the tip of her nose. "Do not forget our staunch private army, love," he said gently.

"Every man-jack and woman-jill of them is panting to serve their laird, from Fredricks and McLeod to young spy Colin, furious because the Talons don't visit the village and give him his chance to catch them at their skulduggery. Then there's Miss Alford, who informs me that the lady Désirée's garments are much too gaudy for a *lady*, and Polly, who is trying to attract the Talon's groom, in order to ferret out the background of the precious pair."

Matilda was much struck. "That's rather a good plan."

The major shook his head. "It is a very bad plan," he corrected. "Your little maid has even less nous than you have. Ian Wallace is upset—fashed, I believe is his word—over the daft wee lassie. I have ordered him to keep her so busy she won't have time to get into trouble."

Smoothing the frown on his wife's forehead with strong, calloused fingers, the major murmured, "I do not underestimate the power of loyal servants," then spoiled it by saying, "in fact, I positively quake at the thought of the harebrained schemes they are concocting at this very instant. If only they do not decide to murder Talon in his bed! As for Polly, she needs to mature a little, but Ian will keep her safe. But who will keep *me* safe, with the whole staff so busy stravaging about in my defense?" He put on an air of apprehension so convincing that the girl's lips pulled into a smile in spite of her anxiety.

"You are past praying for!" Matilda tried to sound stern, but the cowed look he immediately adopted betrayed her and she chuckled. "How can you coax me into laughter when we are in such terrible straits? We should be plotting, scheming, conniving for the downfall and ousting of the pretenders, but instead you are making jokes!"

"You don't like my sense of humor?" the major protested with such a crestfallen expression that Matilda did not know whether to comfort him or give him a scolding for ill-timed levity. As she frowned up into his laughing silver eyes, she knew suddenly exactly what she wanted to do.

She did it.

A blissful few minutes later the major stood back, releasing her from his sturdy grasp.

"Now *that*," he said with no trace of levity at all, "was a vote of confidence!"

Following the major's instructions, Miss Alford and Matilda wrote out invitations to every bigwig in the county, beginning with the Reverend Cameron, his faithful presbyters and their wives, and not even omitting the Earl of Cullan, who had not spoken to anyone but his gillie in twenty years. He had been old Willum's fiercest enemy. He was thought by many to be senile.

At the raised eyebrows of everyone who was within hearing distance—almost the whole staff, since the major had given his orders in the kitchen during the servants' dinner hour—he explained that he was willing to wager his blunt that the old glaikster was far from senile and had probably nosed out every scrap of news about the most exciting thing that had happened in the neighborhood in the last forty years.

While admiring his growing command of Scottish dialect, Matilda had strong reservations against adding to their problems by the introduction of another controversial element.

"What if he . . . ?" she began doubtfully.

"Cuts up rough?" teased the major. "Or cuts *us* entirely—doesna' show his front?" He had given her his broad brogue, to the servants' delight. "Nay, lassie, t'auld skelpin wouldna' permit himsel' to miss our *coup*—that means to capsize or dump—an upset," he explained with a scholarly pride that had the maids giggling. "Whoever wins—us or the pretenders—it bids fair to be a massacre. Think how highly satisfying that will be to the worst enemy the late unlamented laird ever had! Whichever of us claimants wins, it'll be a mortification to the auld laird, who didn't want any man, living or dead, to get one bawbee of his miserly hoard!''

While keenly enjoying his jokes, the servants told one another they'd have to look out for him; increase their vigilance. The pretenders, too, experienced a stirring of unease when the invitations went out, inscribed in Miss Alford's scholarly hand upon the finest paper Factor Wallace could procure at short notice.

To Matilda's surprise, if to no one else's, acceptances began to trickle in. At which point, the major made a fateful decision. He instructed Miss Alford and Polly to accompany their dear mistress to Edinburgh, there to attend her at the finest drapers, or costumiers, or whatever the ladies called such emporiums, and see that she had not only a new, finer wardrobe, more fitting for the laird's wife, but also one special dazzling garment suitable for outfacing the modish Désirée at the coming reception.

When Matilda began to make objections, her husband silenced her with one question: ''Do you not wish to reinforce my consequence at that crucial moment?''

There was no more to be said, although the girl silently set her teeth at the twinkle of sly satisfaction in her domineering husband's handsome face.

Miss Alford and Polly had the sense to hide their amusement at the laird's masterly maneuvering.

The wily fellow even gave Miss Alford a note, properly sealed, to be given to the couturier during their visit.

''It probably contains money,'' Miss Alford soothed her curious pupil. ''Do not worry, my dear, I beg of you. Your husband is a man of many parts. He knows how to do all that is proper and right.''

Since it would be treason to object to this encomium, the girl perforce agreed. But there was still anxiety buried deep in her mind. Chiefly on account of a glint of humor that she sometimes surprised in the warm silver eyes of her maddening, adorable husband when he looked at her. This was no time for joking!

In the event, the first part of their sortie into the metropolis of Edinburgh went very well. Miss Alford, establishing her small party in the finest hotel, had no difficulty in getting directions to the best dress emporium in the city. And the actual purchasing was a sheer joy: the trying on, the taking off in order to don even lovelier costumes—the *decisions*! It was a demiparadise! Toward the end of the daylong session, when the choices had been made and even the great gown, suitable for a dramatic confrontation with Désirée, had been chosen, Matilda remembered the envelope the major had given her governess. While Miss Alford delivered it to the modiste, Matilda took a long, final look at the great gown before carefully handing it to a flattering assistant. It was truly magnificent, more gorgeous than any dress Matilda had ever seen, even on her mama on a royal reception night. The demeaning thought rose in the girl's mind that this impressive garment would be wearing her, rather than the reverse. I shall be lost in its splendor, she worried. Sunk without trace. The lavish creation was more gorgeous than anything Désirée had yet flaunted. Of course, it was most likely she had several truly startling dresses in reserve. For the major's sake, Matilda must wear this *coup de théâtre*. Matilda stifled her fears and nodded to the assistant.

"Wrap it up! And do not crush it, if you please!"

Smiling blandly, the woman took the gown away. Provincial nobodies, she thought, trying to tell Maggie Smith her business! That dress will be a disaster on that child!

Getting the message of the smile clearly, Matilda set her jaw. The business of the war against the pretenders was weakening her resolve. Courage, Matilda! she said. Remember the meaning of your name!

The party of weary, satisfied females returned to the inn

with devout assurances ringing in their ears from the modiste that all the costumes would be delivered to their hotel in good time before their carriage left for the north the next day. Although they had planned to talk until a late hour, discussing strategies to assist the laird, they were all so exhausted by the important work they had accomplished that they cravenly fell asleep in mid-discussion.

Disaster struck the following morning.

They had elected to break their fast in their own room and had found the meal to be more than adequate. Then, dressed à la mode and eager to return to the castle, they had issued down the main stairway and into the entrance hall at the front of the inn.

Matilda's first warning of the disaster came when Miss Alford, proudly leading her small party toward the front doors, paused so abruptly that Matilda and Polly, lagging behind for a final glimpse of the stylish building, bumped into her rigid figure.

Immediately concerned, Matilda caught at Miss Alford's shoulder and asked, "Is something wrong? Are you hurt?"

The governess whirled, grasping the girl by one arm and hissing at Polly, "Cover for us! Follow behind us to block the view!" Without further explanation, she pulled the alarmed Matilda toward the kitchen at the back of the building.

Quite aware of a small commotion occurring behind them, Miss Alford led the two girls quickly out of the kitchen and around the outside of the inn to the stables. There, to the intense relief of the governess, Tom Coachman was just preparing to tool the laird's comfortable carriage around to the front of the inn to pick up his passengers.

Without any ceremony at all, Miss Alford pushed her two charges into the coach ahead of her, and, stopping only long enough to snap at Tom Coachman, "Do not permit *anyone* to halt you!'' she swung into the carriage with a lithe grace that impressed both girls. But there was more.

"Keep your heads down, both of you!'' she commanded. *"It is Lord Mountavon—and the Earl of Tark!"*

Chapter Sixteen

The ride home was a nightmare. Tom Coachman had responded with commendable alacrity to Miss Alford's frightened appeal for speed. It seemed to Matilda that they jolted
through the great city and out onto the open road in a very
short time indeed.

It also occurred to her that it might be easy for her father
and the earl to follow their desperate flight; surely many persons would recall the passage of such a handsome vehicle,
four splendid horses at full gallop.

She braced herself with both hands against the jolting of
the carriage and made a searching scrutiny of the faces of her
companions. Both countenances were pale and drawn with
fear. For the first time since she had so gladly embarked upon
this adventure, Miss Alford looked every day of her age. She
was staring blindly ahead, the fingers of one hand plucking
at her lips. Polly, terrified by the magnitude of the disaster,
had her eyes fixed in agonized inquiry on her young mistress's face.

And at that moment Matilda understood her duty. She was
the laird's wife. No man could put asunder those whom God
had joined. She took courage in the loving determination of
her major to protect her from just such a threat as this.

So: What was her course of action to be?

As the laird's wife, she must take control of this flight and keep it from degenerating into utter rout. Consciously relaxing her cramped muscles, Matilda summoned up a smile. No matter that it was a poor excuse for the spontaneous merriment that had sparkled in her face for the past few days: it was a smile.

"Dear Alfer, Polly—listen to me!"

Two pairs of eyes fixed eagerly on her at that quiet, confident command. Polly perked up at once. Her dear Lady was going to make all things right, as she had so sensibly done during their earlier flight to the Dodd kitchen and then to Scotland. And now she had the major to back her up! Polly had a world of respect for the major.

Miss Alford's response was not so rapid. It took a few moments for her to pull herself out of the morass of fear and, yes, hatred she felt for Matilda's cruel, selfish parents. But she met the loving challenge in the wide golden eyes and thought, irrelevantly, how much prettier her dear pupil was looking these days, with good food, and interesting work, and a loving major. The clear soft skin had a glow she had never seen on it before, and the beautiful eyes were sparkling now with that intent, wily stare that characterized one of Matilda's determined moods. She had seen and admired that light before, as evidence that no amount of callous neglect or cruel indifference could crush the child's gallant spirit. We have need of all your courage now, dearest child, she thought.

When she was sure she had the attention of both women, Matilda said quietly, "We will get to the castle before my father and the earl. If, in fact, that is their destination."

No one replied to that too-hopeful suggestion. It was obvious that, having tracked the runaway this far, the two noblemen would hardly give up at the moment of success.

Matilda went on, "Dear Alfer, did either of them see you, do you think?"

Miss Alford did not try to temper the wind to the shorn

lamb. "Tark was consulting with the host. I am sure your father glimpsed us. There was a small commotion as we ran away."

Matilda drew in a deep breath. You are the laird's wife, she reminded herself. Your people depend upon you. He depends upon you! First comfort; then command. Am I learning strategy from you, my dear lord? Or is it tactics?

"Thanks to you, dear Alfer, we escaped. Had it not been for your timely warning, I would have gone blundering down into their arms!" This thought being too devastating for her hearers, Matilda quickly passed to the commanding tone. "Now we must make sure that we reach the castle well in advance of our pursuers. The major must have every possible advantage in setting up his defenses." She ventured a rallying laugh. "You both know how very good our major is at defense!"

This sally brought answering smiles to the lips of her companions. Miss Alford had so far collected her wits as to be able to respond with one of her familiar aphorisms.

"Forewarned," she said crisply, "is forearmed. Yes, my dear, I have perfect confidence in the laird. I just wish he had not invited half the countryside to that reception!"

Polly raised an unexpected voice. "That won't daunt the major," she affirmed stoutly. "He'll just play up all the better with an audience."

For some reason, this tribute to the major's skill in skulduggery delighted both of Polly's companions and relieved the tension of the moment. In the face of such confidence, Matilda chided herself for her own lack of faith.

The next hour was spent in proposing wild schemes that the proposers soon realized were absurd but served to keep fear at bay and to maintain a strong, confident attitude. When Tom Coachman drew up at a small inn for refreshment of passengers and horses, the ladies were very pleased to climb down with his respectful assistance and to enjoy a restorative snack and freshen themselves for the rest of the long drive.

"I am confident we are well in advance of the attackers," Matilda kept to the military terms they had all been using. "Their carriage was not ready to leave, as ours was. In fact, it was probably being unharnessed at that very moment. By the time they could have had it prepared again, we were well out of Edinburgh. It may take them days to find us," she finished hopefully.

Although the more worldly-wise Miss Alford could not agree—for was not her own signature and that of "Lady Bruce" clearly inscribed upon the host's book? The one instantly recognizable, the other a clear lead to the desired goal—she sensibly forebore to mention such uncomfortable facts. What good would it do? She had a deep-seated fear of the ability of such noblemen as Mountavon, and especially Tark, to obtain instant and effective service and to see a name that was directly beneath their noses. However, she only nodded and said vaguely, "Safe bind, safe find."

Catching the confusion in their expressions, Miss Alford gave her first real smile since the beginning of their flight. "That aphorism popped into my mind, I think, because it has the words *safe*—for us—and *bind*—for them. As the poet William Cowper has said, 'To combat may be glorious, and success/ Perhaps may crown us; but *to fly is safe.*' Or, to put it in less poetic language, 'He who fights and runs away, will live to fight another day.' That sounds cowardly, I know, but I just can't wait to fly to the castle and warn our dear major!"

This brought the heartiest laughter of the day, and even a tear or two, which refreshed the ladies very much.

When they reached the castle, they stopped only long enough to praise and thank their coachman before going to seek out the laird. He listened to every agonized detail of their desperate report without comment, merely holding his arm around Matilda with firm reassurance.

This masculine support was so welcome to the girl that she snuggled happily against his large torso with a sigh of relief.

"Later, love," the rascal had the effrontery to whisper, while keeping his attention focused steadily upon Miss Alford's rendition of their tale. His naughty comment had, however, the effect of restoring Matilda's poise. She smiled up into his beloved face, feeling such a surge of love and confidence that she leaned up and kissed the closest part of that face available, his strong jaw.

Ignoring the deep thrust of pleasure this gesture gave him, the major said, "It is interesting that we are to entertain so many of the local gentry tomorrow night. How fortunate, in view of the imminent arrival of Lord Mountavon, that we had some of them as witnesses to our wedding! I would back the Reverend Cameron against Lord Mountavon and a *brace* of Tarks."

"The Talons!" gasped Matilda, remembering their chief antagonists with dismay. "What will they say?"

"Does it matter?" The laird kissed her with firm, warm lips and then pushed her gently toward Miss Alford. "I would suggest that you ladies repair at once to your rooms to rest after your exhausting experience. Fredricks shall send up tea and sandwiches; the maids are alerted to fill the tubs with hot water; and your purchases, which I have, no doubt have made a sizable dent in my fortune, will be in your rooms as soon as you are. Go, now! Rest and remember: *'The will to do; the soul to dare'!*"

His smile is like . . . like sunshine, thought the dazzled Matilda. If only he had called me Merielle! But it seemed that that love-name was to be reserved for their most intimate and precious moments, and the girl accepted that.

"We shall do the laird proud tomorrow night!" she said firmly.

Be sure her companions agreed.

Chapter Seventeen

Just before she began to dress for dinner that evening, Matilda discovered a box resting provocatively upon her bed. It bore the stamp of the Edinburgh modiste. Had not Polly unpacked and carefully hung up all their purchases? Was this a special treat, a surprise from the major? Eagerly the girl unwrapped the garment and held it up to her astonished gaze.

It was a dress—and obviously meant for her, with its beautiful, soft, white material and small size. But it was . . . *plain*, almost severe in cut, the style rigidly austere. Could it be—a nightgown? But surely not, with that sumptuous yet restrained richness of material. Matilda regarded the severely beautiful garment with a puzzled smile, then hung it carefully in the armoire beside the other new garments they had purchased. She placed it as far as possible from the great dress. She did not want the major's special gift to suffer comparisons with that lavish opulence!

Resolving to thank her generous husband at the first opportunity, she closed the armoire and went to look for him. She could not find him. One of the footmen (promoted from the ranks of the London grooms Bruce had hired), informed her that he had seen his lairdship strolling toward the South Tower.

Matilda thanked him and headed that way herself. Why

would the major be seeking a conference with the Talons? Could he not wait to discuss whatever it was with them at the dinner table shortly? Was there an emergency? Her alarm grew greater as she approached the Tower and saw no sign of him. For some reason: caution, fear of what she might hear, see, whatever, the girl entered by the small rear door and proceeded up the back, servants', stairway. She did not make any particular effort to be silent, but her soft slippers moved along the narrow stone hallway so quietly that no sound alerted the Talons that they had a visitor.

As she overheard the first words through the partly opened bedroom door, the girl froze back against the rough stone wall and held her breath.

"—whole thing is falling apart in our hands!" Hubert was whining. "He must have more support in the district than we were told or he wouldn't be bringing them all here tomorrow night!"

In a voice whose vicious coldness Matilda had never heard before, Désirée said, "Stop sniveling, you fool! The soldier is just what we expected, brave enough to charge a square single-handed, but without enough brains to know when he's outmaneuvered! He's just putting up a bold front, Bert. You know our plan will work. Every important person in the neighborhood hates him. The shopkeeper told you that!"

"What if Wallace was wrong?" asked Hubert petulantly. "I don't like the look in that soldier's eye, I tell you!"

Désirée said, in a softer, coaxing voice, "Come on, Bert! You've trusted me this far, trust me all the way! When I'm done with that blockhead, he'll be out in the cold and on his way back to the army. Now you must do just as I told you. Tonight, after dinner, I will engage to get him over here to my bedroom. I'll use one of the old dodges, and I promise you he won't suspect a thing. I can keep him here long enough for you to search the muniment room for any paper that might prove his right to the castle, and destroy it. Then you can hide

142

that document we had prepared in London—someplace where he won't be likely to stumble onto it until we're ready.''

"It won't work," said Hubert pessimistically. "It's a mad scheme! Too many chances of discovery—!"

"Then I'll just have to pull the old trick, won't I? It never fails," and she gave a laugh that made Matilda's skin chill. "Remember that young lordling in Paris? His papa was eager enough to meet our price!"

Hubert was proving recalcitrant. "What if it doesn't work? We shall have wrecked our chances for sure. I say we should wait to see what the nobs think of us tomorrow night. If they choose to back us, there'll be no need for your nasty little games."

There was a long silence. Matilda held her breath. They must not discover her here!

Finally Désirée spoke. "Very well. I'll wait until after the famous reception tomorrow night. But I warn you, Bert, if the local bigwigs do not fall on your neck and kiss you, I intend playing my own game on the major later."

There was a sound of movement within the room. Matilda whirled and raced on tiptoe along the hallway and down the back stairs.

Where was the major? She must tell him what she had heard!

This proved curiously difficult to do.

For one thing, it took a long time to find him. No one seemed to know where he was, not even Fredricks, although Matilda suspected the old man knew more than he was telling. Since she had no doubts about the butler's loyalty, Matilda forced herself to be content with his polite evasions, merely warning him crossly to tell the absent gentleman, when he surfaced, that this was no time to be playing least-in-sight.

Fredricks smiled and advised her that Miss Alford would not approve of her using cant phrases.

Eventually she ran her quarry to earth in the muniment room. Closing and locking the door behind her, she advanced upon the major with finger to lips.

The wretch immediately assumed a frightened stance, his eyes glinting with amusement.

He was so absurd, with his huge soldier's body cringing behind the desk in mimic fear, that Matilda had to laugh.

"I'm not going to hurt you, you great—uh—"

"Skelpin?" suggested the major. "Limmer? Danderheaded fautor?"

"I shall not," said Matilda firmly, "ask what any of those Scottish words means."

The major threw back his head in one of the open shouts of laughter Matilda so much enjoyed hearing. "Truly, they are quite—proper," he managed to say. "Homespun, perhaps . . . " His wide grin teased her to join the fun.

But Matilda had grave matters to discuss and moved toward him around the desk, so her voice would not carry.

The villain approached her hopefully. "You've come to seduce me, wife? In the middle of the day? In the muniment room?"

Matilda, properly incensed by his determined effort to play the fool, was still not proof against the laughing charm of her incorrigible lover. As he folded her close to him, she allowed herself the nourishment of one kiss before whispering against his ear, "I overheard the Talons plotting in their room. Do let me tell you their plans, so you can prepare to frustrate them!"

The major gave her one final hug and then put her away from him. "Yes, you are right, mighty battle-maid! Now is not the time for dalliance. What exactly did they say?"

Matilda repeated it, as closely as she could remember.

The major considered, frowning.

"She wanted to get me into her bedroom tonight, while Bert searched this room for my documents. He intended to substitute fake papers that he had prepared in London, which would destroy my credit when 'discovered' by him or his agents."

"But Hubert overruled her," Matilda reminded him. "He is certain the important great families of the district will accept him rather than yourself as the true heir."

Her major frowned at her with exasperation. "How can the opinion of a group of provincial old fuddy-duds change my legal rights? Even if Hubert could rouse the whole county against us, I should be affirmed in my ownership by due process of law, no matter how long—"

"But that's just it!" protested the girl. "You said yourself it could take months, *years*, to win a legal battle! In the meantime, the Talons could rob the estate, squeeze it dry—and disappear!"

The major stared down into her troubled golden eyes. Then he shook his dark head. Her flame of loyalty warmed him to the very center of his being. But she was so young, so open. . . . He dared not reveal the plan he had devised. She would not be able to conceal it from his wily enemies, alert for any clue or sign of weakness. For her own sake, for her safety, she must be told nothing the pretenders could use.

There was only one course a soldier could pursue.

"Merielle." It was not a name he used lightly; they both knew that.

"Yes, Robert?"

"Do you trust me?"

"With my life. My soul." Eyes held steady and loving on his.

"My request is this: that you live the next few days as my loving and beloved wife, as Matilda and Merielle in one dear body—as *yourself*. Trusting me. With your own precious dignity and pride. Without fear—"

Carefully he watched the loving light glow in those beautiful eyes, the warmth and sweetness of his wife's smile. And then Matilda surprised him.

"For the next few days, you prefer Merielle to Matilda, I can see that! You soldiers! One would think a battle-maid might be a worthy recruit, but you want to have all the fun yourself!"

Relief and joy mingled in his laughter. How had he been lucky enough to find her, in all the world? His arm around her slender body pressed her painfully close, as wordlessly he sought to find some way of telling her how much she meant to him.

And again she surprised him.

"You'll win this skirmish, I know," she said softly. "But I must also advise you, sir, that win or lose, you cannot get rid of this battle-maid. Our paths are one. And so I shall tell our children, when we have them."

Silent in her arms, as she was now in his, the major blessed his good fortune.

Chapter Eighteen

In spite of Matilda's fears, the evening went off without overt violence. True, there were a number of subtle digs from Désirée, all of them skillfully designed to depress the pretensions of the little child-wife, but these failed of their effect. All Matilda had to do, when attention was slyly called to her *corsage manqué*, was to cast a gentle glance over her tormentor's too-lavish bosom, thrusting its way out of the encasing satin, and smile. Matilda realized she had, in a real sense, grown up that afternoon in the muniment room with her husband.

She only hoped the major knew what he was doing!

The next day was a chaos of preparation for the reception. Grooms, riding back and forth from the village for last-minute necessities, aroused so much interest among the populace that a straggling line of those who could safely neglect their current business formed along Glenholme village's one street to cheer the riders. It was the most exciting day in recent history. And, warned by the merchant Wallace, they were aware of great and possibly catastrophic changes at Castle Glenholme. On that matter, the village was divided. The families of all those hired by the Sassenach major were apprehensive that he might be unseated by the beautiful pair of claimants. The shopkeeper's wife and younger son, whose loyalty had obviously been won by the major and whose elder son, Ian, was so delighted with his new position as factor to the castle, were clearly opposed to the merchant's campaign against the Sassenach. Wallace himself lost no opportunity to inform anyone within hearing that the Englishman would get his comeuppance that night, when the local bigwigs would put him in his place once and for all—outside the castle!

"And where will that leave Ian?" the exasperated Mrs. Wallace finally demanded. "On the outside also, without the work he loves! Whiles, Mr. Wallace, I think you are daft!"

"Dinna' whine, wumman," advised her spouse. "Donal Wallace hasna' lost his wits! I have the golden boy's word on it. None in the village shall suffer for this night's work!"

At the castle, the drawbridge was down, the flambeaux and torches alight, the Great Hall adorned and ready for the expected arrivals.

If only they all come! prayed Matilda. The Major must not be hurt!

Every man and woman in the castle, with the exception of the Talons, was on the stretch to do the laird proud. There was a general, carefully suppressed fear that the soldier might be outclassed by the devious pretenders, and the staff were keeping a very sharp eye on the proceedings. If any effort of theirs could save the day for Robert Bruce, it would be made.

Matilda, coming downstairs after a maddening session with Miss Alford and Polly, felt literally at her wit's end. It had taken the combined efforts of the three of them to get Matilda into the great dress, and the girl decided despairingly that it wasn't worth it. No matter how high she held her head, no matter how she braced her shoulders, she could not *wear* the costume. As she had feared in Edinburgh, the too-elaborate, heavily-adorned garment was *wearing her*. When she reached the Great Hall and prepared to face the Talons and the major, she was ready to admit that she had failed her darling.

One look at Désirée made her fears a reality.

The woman had on a gown of gold satin, so heavily beaded with brilliants that it cast a shine about her person. From the too-tight bodice, her bounteous breasts threatened momentarily to burst forth; her bright golden hair gleamed in the light of the hundreds of candles above her in the chandelier. Her face was skillfully, if heavily, painted in the latest maquillage from Paris. In a word, she was *formidable*. And Hubert! Not even Paris at the height of the Sun King's glory could have presented anything so elaborate, so eye-catching, so overpowering! The golden youth truly glittered.

Matilda cast one anguished glance at her husband. He, at least, looked every inch the laird, she thought. In the dress tartan and kilt of his clan, his dark head proudly lifted above strong, broad shoulders, he did not stand out as did his rival, but he made her proud to be his wife. His smile warmed her heart.

Then he was coming toward her, catching up a glass of sherry from a tray as he approached.

"To your eyes, milady!" he proposed, snatching up a second glass to make his toast.

And then it happened. For some reason his foot caught on the venerable old carpet, and the sherry from the glass he had intended to offer her shot out and drenched the front of the great dress.

There was a frozen silence on the part of the servants and the Talons and then . . .

Désirée's laugh shrilled out, to be followed at once by an abject apology from the major.

"My darling! What can I say? You must go up at once and put on another of those pretty dresses you got in Edinburgh! I know! To show that you forgive my gaucherie, please wear the dress I gave you." The last words were whispered against her ear, as her dismayed husband kissed her cheek in a bid for forgiveness.

Matilda squared her shoulders, smiled, and said in a small, clear voice, "Not quite a disaster, darling, although that modiste would probably think so! Pray excuse me, Miss Talon, Mr. Talon, while I go to change."

She got herself out of the Great Hall and back to the laird's bedchamber without breaking down, the memory of her husband's proud smile sustaining her. Miss Alford had gone back to her own rooms to freshen up for the demanding evening ahead, but Polly was still in the bedroom, tidying up. Her face, when she saw the huge brown stain on the elaborate dress, would at any other time have been enough to make Matilda laugh. Now Matilda said briefly, "An accident. Help me into something else."

"He didn't miss much of it." Gloomily the maid surveyed the enormous stain. "Which dress do you want?"

"The major wishes me to wear the dress he bought as a surprise for me," Matilda advised her. She tried to relieve the shock on Polly's features with a mild jest. "I had no idea he was so determined that I should wear his gift."

This remark seemed to increase the maid's unhappiness. Matilda hastened to assure Polly she had just been joking, and they got to the business of removing the stained costume without further talk.

When at length the plain, rather austere dress of the major's choice had been donned, both girls turned to survey the results in the huge mirror that had been another of the soldier's gifts to his wife. Polly's expression began to lighten gradually.

"I wouldn't have believed it, milady, but you look real *pretty*," she whispered. "It suits you better than that other one."

"It is more youthful," said Matilda between set teeth. "I appear to be about fifteen-years-old. And *hideously* prim!"

Polly, knowing that set look of old, said nothing more while she brushed out the overelaborate coiffure Miss Alford had decreed obligatory for the great dress and put up Matilda's soft brown hair in the simple manner that was habitual for her.

"Brings out your eyes, that does," she announced, standing back to view the results of her work.

Peering tensely into the mirror, Matilda took courage from the one good thing that had come out of the debacle. The simpler hairstyle *did* emphasize her eyes, making them glow large and golden in her small face. But the dress—! It was high-necked, almost virginal in appearance, but that was not the worst feature. It seemed coldly austere in spite of the pure delicacy of its material and style. Despairingly she recalled the gleaming creation of the bosomy Désirée and admitted that no one would give the laird's wife a second glance when presented with that lavish décolletage.

She caught Polly's commiserating glance and held her head high. "Thank you, Polly! Now you must go down to the Hall and join the others. I know you do not want to miss . . . to miss . . . " Her voice faltered. "The great occasion," she finished firmly.

And went down bravely to stand beside her husband.

She had hardly had time to receive the triumphant scrutiny of Désirée and the warmly reassuring smile of the major before Fredricks announced the first of the visitors. Predictably it was the Reverend George Cameron, who was proving himself a friend in need. He was accompanied by the Mac-Donnells, and they were followed almost immediately by the two other couples who had attended the major's first dinner.

The major quickly arranged his party in a reception line, with the minister at his left shoulder to introduce each guest. Next to himself the major had placed Matilda, to her great joy and relief. At least she would have the comfort of his warm presence to sustain her under the critical or scornful glances she was sure to receive from the high sticklers.

I must not forget, she told herself, that I am here to support my husband, however inadequately I may do it. She raised her small head proudly and prepared to meet the attack. She needed all her courage, since at her right shoulder was the glittering golden figure of the claimant. She could even detect a strong waft of perfume from his person as he waved a lace kerchief idly before his face.

He gave her a malicious look. "How unfortunate that your husband spilled the wine on your *good* dress," he commiserated.

Matilda felt an unfamiliar stir of malice. She gave him a wide, golden stare, and said ingenuously, "But who would bother to glance at me when they have you and your sister to look at—*Bert*?"

Hubert shot a quick frowning glance at her, but the guests were moving down the line toward him, and he needed every ounce of charm and guile he could dredge up to impress them with his superior fitness for the role of laird. He darted one quick look at Désirée, so voluptuous in her dazzling gown, and then prepared to win over the local gentry. His absolute confidence that he could do so was revealed in his rather smug little smile.

Matilda turned her eyes toward the major. He had been chatting easily with the MacDonnells, but almost as though there was an agreement between them, he turned and smiled at his wife at that moment.

"Dearest, you remember the MacDonnells?"

As the couple advanced, smiling, Matilda beamed at them. "How could I forget the guests who made our wedding such a warm and welcoming event?" she said sincerely. "I felt as though I had come home."

Lady Margaret gave her a glance of sharp approval and shook her hand firmly. "You do Glenholme proud," was all she said, but it was enough to reestablish the girl's confidence. Heartened by the quiet acceptance of the Mac-Donnells and George Cameron, Matilda began the task made inevitable by her position in the line: the introduction of the pretender and his sister to all the guests.

Hubert was playing the young laird in dashing style. His beautiful face wore a charming smile; his hair gleamed in the light of the candles; his golden coat shimmered; his perfume wafted in a cloud about him. Matilda was secretly pleased to see a faint frown on MacDonnell's heavy countenance. Perhaps he did not approve of so much perfume for a man? But then, she thought with a sigh, one glance at the voluptuous Désirée and all would be forgiven! She leaned forward and made the introduction as graciously as she was able. Désirée cooed and smiled languorously from under her darkened eyelashes, flattering the lord of the MacDonnells. To Matilda's astonishment, Désirée passed over Lady Margaret with the merest formal grimace. A tiny bud of hope pushed itself up in the girl's mind, but she corrected herself sternly. It is the laird they will judge, not a sister or a wife!

She was not left free to indulge either hopes or fears during the next half hour. Surprisingly the guests continued to arrive. Since they were gentlefolk by birth and training, they were equally polite to both claimants to the title, but the avid curiosity that had brought them here could not be disguised. None were so openly cordial as Lord and Lady MacDonnell had been, but each greeted the major and Hubert with cool courtesy. Hubert was in his glory. His charming smile embraced everyone; he preened and flattered and flirted in the way that had served him so well in Paris, Vienna, Rome, and London. The major, to Matilda's deep unease, did none of these things. He was, she thought, even quieter than usual, with no faintest glint of that delightful humor that made his wide smile so devastating. Had he given up the fight? Or was he too proud to stoop to wily seduction in order to conquer?

The Great Hall became more crowded. Delicious food was displayed upon well-lighted tables; footmen in neat livery moved among the guests offering drink. The voices of Hubert and Désirée rose above the babble of the crowd. The evening began to look like a triumph for the Talons. And then Fredricks announced, ''The Right Honorable Earl of Cullan!'' with incredulity carefully concealed.

Standing in the enormous arched doorway, staring around the Great Hall as though it were a kennel, was a man almost as large as the major. His features were nearly obscured by a heavy beard, and a glengarry cap rode on the bushy hair. His dress plaid was rumpled, but he was, Matilda decided, one of the two most impressive figures in the Hall.

At his shoulder, looking even more disheveled than his laird, stood a man who could only be the earl's gillie. He, too, was glaring around at the assembled company as though to dare them to approach his master. Was their presence a sign of goodwill or a portent of disaster, Matilda wondered, moving toward Bruce.

Startled, she noticed McLeod enter behind the newcomers and move unobtrusively into a position at the major's shoulder. Had the situation been less crucial, the girl might have grinned at the primitive males squaring off in preparation for battle. Bless you, McLeod, she thought. We're *all* behind him, whatever happens!

An apprehensive silence gradually fell upon the gathering as one after another of the guests perceived who it was who had entered. A subdued susurrus swept the great room. Then again all conversation ceased as the major, with McLeod at his shoulder, moved toward the unexpected guest. The big soldier stopped in front of the glowering Lord Cullan and held out his hand.

''I bid you welcome to Glenholme, Lord Cullan,'' he said quietly, but his deep voice was clear throughout the silent room. "You do me honor. May I present my wife, Lady Matilda?"

Be sure that Matilda was at his side in a swift but dignified walk. She smiled gently up into the frightening, bearded face and extended her own hand. "I bid you welcome in my laird's name," she said, as quietly as her husband had spoken.

For an agonizing moment, Matilda was afraid that the huge, savage Scotsman would not even speak to them, much less accept the extended hands. His knife-sharp blue eyes raked them both from head to foot, then went beyond them to the Talons, who, led by Désirée, were approaching rapidly.

"And these," with a nod of the big, hairy head under the glengarry cap, "are the Sassenachs? You were a fool to give them house-room." His voice grated as though it had not been used in years.

Désirée, coming up fast, heard the comment and gasped with outrage. Recollecting herself in time, she put on her most seductive pout. "No, your lairdship, *we* are the true heirs, and *these*," her heavily-ringed hand indicated the major and Matilda, "are the Sassenachs."

The earl looked her over as though she were a prize animal being offered for sale. His searching scrutiny took in every detail of the voluptuous figure in its blazing costume. "I ken well what *you are*," he grated. "But you're not the other claimant. Can't he speak for himself?"

Hubert almost pushed Désirée aside in his effort to present himself to the old autocrat. He was flustered, completely at a loss. He had heard of the earl of Cullan but had not visualized such an overpowering, savage presence. The hairy nobleman dwarfed by his personality as much as by his physical aspect nearly every other man in the Great Hall, yet he was carelessly dressed and uncouth in manner—and even smelled of sweat and horses! Distracted by this unexpected confrontation, Hubert waved his scented handkerchief in front of his nose.

The earl laughed.

"You are the Sassenach," he said. "I can smell it on you." Without another word to Hubert, he turned to the major and Matilda and took both their still-extended hands in his.

"Perhaps now we shall have a sensible laird at Glenholme Castle," he announced, loudly enough to be heard by everyone in the huge hall. "I knew your grandfather before auld Willum drove him away to England. He was my friend, a good steady man. You have a look of him."

To Matilda's trembling joy, the other males among the guests came up with smiling faces to surround the accepted laird and the man who had confirmed his status. Fredricks and the footmen hastened to serve filled glasses for the expected toast. The Earl of Cullan scrutinized McLeod with his sharp gaze.

"Ye've got a prime gillie there, Bruce," he admitted. "At yer shoulder the minute I entered the hall. Ye may present him."

"Lord Cullan, may I present Sergeant Ronal McLeod," Bruce drew McLeod forward with a nod. Shoulders straight, face imperturbable, the sergeant made his salute.

Cullan grinned. "Crusty, isn't he? Willna' truckle, nor give an inch! I like that." He moved his head to indicate the silent man at his own shoulder. "This is Conal," he said. "My own man."

The two servants nodded so warily that the earl chuckled again. Then he raised his glass and shouted *"Bruce!"* bowing and holding up the glass in salute toward the major before he downed its contents in one great gulp.

The shout was taken up by the whole assemblage, with the not surprising exception of the Talons. Hubert, standing ignored in his inappropriate finery, seemed unable to think of any course of action that would not leave him looking more foolish than he did at the moment. His golden beauty seemed dim and blemished; with his face white under the maquillage, he looked every day of his real age.

Désirée was made of sterner stuff. Rather unwisely she thrust herself into the crowd of males surrounding the newly acclaimed laird and his surprising sponsor.

"I think we should talk this over," she began, rather stridently, and then, becoming aware of the raised eyebrows on several faces near her, she moderated her tone. "Major Bruce is as much a Sassenach as my brother and myself, and I demand—"

It was the wrong word to use in this situation. Hubert heard it with a sense of angry alarm. Even Désirée was at once aware that she had made a disastrous false step. She looked about her with her most seductive smile, but it was too late and the wrong weapon. The earl summed it up.

"Get rid of these spongers, Bruce," he advised. "They give the castle a bad name." He inclined his hairy head, crowned with the old glengarry, toward the quietly glowing Matilda. "I see ye've enough kennin to get yersel' a gude wife, mon," he lapsed into the broad burr. "She'll gie ye strong bairns and bonnie wee lassies, an' we'll see gude life in Glenholme at last." He raised his glass to the blushing Matilda.

The dazzled girl could not believe the evidence of her senses. After the agonies they all—yes, even the major, now smiling so serenely—had endured, could the problem have been solved with such apparent ease? She was almost afraid to believe it, lest some other menace creep upon them unnoticed. Her husband bent over her, his smiling silver eyes so close to her own that her vision blurred.

"Your eyes are crossed, gude wife," he grinned wickedly. "But I like your dress. It suits ma prim Scots sense o' what's fittin' for the laird's wife. Ye may thank me properly for it later."

The truth burst upon the girl like a stroke of lightning. Her major had judged the temper and prejudices of the Scottish community more clearly than the Talons had done. But could she ever forgive him for the wicked trick he had played upon her, deliberately spilling wine on the great dress in order to get her into his own sober—and correct!—choice? Of course, she realized, that naughty trick had accomplished two goals: It had gotten her into the modest dress, and it had given the Talons a powerful, if false, sense of their own superiority. Put them off-guard.

Oh, that tricksy, manipulating, quirkish, devious *creature*! Waiting for anger to flame up, Matilda felt instead a great surge of joyous laughter. How she loved him, the rascal! Would he always be like this, teasing and joking and regarding her with those glinting, fun-filled silver eyes? Waiting for her response to some new, outrageous ploy? She turned exasperated, delighted eyes upon his smiling face.

At that moment, Fredricks, white of face, hurried up to the besotted pair and whispered, in a voice of doom, ''The Earl of Tark . . . Mountavon . . . ! They demand to speak to the laird!''

Chapter Nineteen

Two Englishmen in modish traveling costume strode into the Great Hall on the heels of Fredricks's announcement. They were exhausted by the long and unpleasant journey they had just endured. Very much out of charity with each other, they still realized that the success of their mission depended upon continued cooperation, at least until they had what they wanted—Matilda. The two men paused involuntarily at the sight of the large number of handsomely dressed men and women who were enjoying the hospitality of the laird of Glenholme and were suddenly very much aware of the rumpled condition of their own clothing.

From the instant he had caught sight of Miss Alford in the finest hostel Edinburgh boasted, Lord Mountavon had been having second thoughts as to the wisdom of this journey. He was a Londoner himself, hated travel of any kind, except a comfortable short jaunt to his club or a favorite gaming hall. The enforced company of the man to whom he was so fatally indebted was abrasive even to his less-than-sensitive nature. In fact, if he could have thought of any other way out of the imbroglio, he would gladly have abandoned Tark and Matilda to their own wretched devices!

It had been the barest glimpse of the old governess that he had caught in that elegant foyer, but he knew he could not have been mistaken. And the way she had turned and scuttled away, herding the other two servants behind her, had confirmed his suspicion. In that one fleeting glimpse, he had not been able to identify Alford's two companions, but her presence there had been clue enough. Unfortunately, while he was acquainting Tark with his discovery, the woman and her companions had made their escape. The earl had made Mountavon's life a misery since then, pointing out not once but many times that the first act of a sensible man would have been to seize the female and hold her until they could force her to tell them where Matilda was hiding.

Since the moment he and Tark had reached the miserable hamlet of Glenholme, only to discover that there was no inn and that they would have to confront Matilda's employer on his own ground at this uncivilized hour or spend the night in the carriage, the situation had begun to acquire the elements of a farce.

They had no need to try to rouse anyone in the village to get directions to their destination. Robert Bruce's home stood out in the darkness like some magic castle from an ancient legend. Lights flamed and bloomed from every tower and turret; great arched windows blazed with color. Even Tark drew in a sharp breath as a turn in the road beside the river revealed the massive structure in all its medieval splendor.

Surely the man who owned this would have no interest in his unattractive daughter, fumed Lord Mountavon. It must be as the Dodd woman had said: Bruce had hired the chit as a cook or a maid! Mountavon set his teeth and hoped that Tark would hold to his bargain. The old roué must indeed be anxious to secure the succession, to go through this difficult journey for so plain and dowerless a female, however nobly born! Well, they were inside the castle, but Mountavon despaired of finding his plain daughter among the throng. God forbid she was actually serving as a maid for this reception!

He scanned the crowd restlessly as he followed Tark into the room.

The earl was looking for their host. It was awkward that neither he nor Mountavon had ever seen the fellow who had brought Matilda to Scotland. A crippled soldier, the Dodd woman had said. What had such a fellow to do with this castle, this company? Tark's eye caught the flash and glitter of a golden dress. Noting it and the voluptuous figure it graced with surprise and admiration, the earl began to feel better. Perhaps in the depths of this wild country, there was game he might pleasurably pursue? He had not thought there could be anything as attractive as this lush, fashionable creature buried in the wilds of the north! Almost immediately he noticed a similarly colorful male figure. The couple stood out from among their more sober fellows like jewels among dross. Easily the smartest and most elegant persons in the vast room, the pair were probably the lord and lady of Glenholme. Tark walked toward them just as a kilted giant advanced from the other side. Tark ignored the big fellow and addressed the golden youth.

"I am the Earl of Tark," he began arrogantly. "Have I the honor of addressing the laird of Glenholme?" His eyes were assessing the daring décolletage of the woman; it was enough to make a man forget that he was here to collect a homely little virgin who would satisfy his need for an heir and yet place no restraints on his preferred way of life.

Instead of the smile of welcome that he had expected or even the cold challenge Mountavon feared, the golden-haired dandy before him frowned petulantly and turned away. The woman stared up into Tark's face with a look of calculated seductiveness that was familiar to Tark.

"We are related to the dead laird," the woman answered him, "but it seems a rival claimant has managed to persuade the local powers that his claim is the better one. We shall be leaving for London in the morning." And good riddance to this benighted place! her bitter expression added.

Tark decided the situation had distinct possibilities, but first he must secure the girl and get his business settled.

At his shoulder, Mountavon had already lost patience with this byplay. He turned to the hovering elderly butler, whom he had by now recognized as the dismissed Fredricks.

"Where is Lady Matilda?" he snapped, his tone promising a bitter reckoning with all treacherous servants and runaway children.

Fredricks drew himself up to his best height and said formally, "I shall discover if Lady Matilda wishes to receive you, milord."

"*Wishes*—?" stammered Lord Mountavon. "What in the devil is *that* supposed to mean?"

"It means," said the major quietly from behind him, "that my wife and I are entertaining our friends and neighbors, and I have no intention of letting two uninvited strangers disrupt the proceedings. You will follow me, if you please, you and your—friend, and tell me what's brought you here."

The laird's tone was enough to enrage a saint, thought Mountavon, but he followed those broad shoulders and the swinging kilt out of the room. It pleased him a little to note that Tark also followed without demur. Somehow one did not wish to come to points with such a massive and cold-voiced antagonist. Mountavon was very much aware of the murmur of interested comment from guests who had witnessed their abrupt departure so short a time after their arrival. It infuriated him to realize that he, George Mountavon, was providing amusement for these Scottish bumpkins. Matilda was piling up a heavy debt! If he had not been well aware of what her life with Tark would be, he might even have beaten her himself for putting him through these last hellish weeks. Well, her punishment, whatever it was, could not start until she was in Tark's hands and the debt safely paid. He hurried to catch up with the arrogant master of this castle. Damn it, the fellow had *agreed* to take the girl out of England without regard for her name or station! He'd pick that bone with him first and then see how arrogant the fellow would be!

The arrogant laird had halted within a small room that was obviously used to transact the estate's business. Fredricks, that treacherous servant, had somehow managed to arrive before them with a pair of lamps, and when, at a nod from the laird, he had placed these on a big desk and left the room, a kilted servant entered and stood by the door in a manner uncomfortably like that of a soldier on guard. What had they got themselves into?

Their unwilling host faced his guests across the heavy desk. He did not ask them to be seated, nor did he offer refreshment to two weary travelers. Barbarian!

"You will state your business with me," he said coldly.

Mountavon's anger stood him in good stead. "I would like the return of my daughter, Matilda, stolen from her family in London," he snapped back, without roundaboutation.

The Earl of Tark snickered. "Well done, Mountavon! I did not know you had it in you! I warn you, though, if he's had her, our bargain is off. You know I specified a virgin." He turned to the laird. "Well, sir, what have you to say to that?"

"To you, I say only that if you open your foul mouth again in my presence, I shall have my servants throw you into the moat." His steel-cold glare gave evidence that he meant every word. When he received no reply from Tark, he turned the metallic gaze upon Mountavon. "Your daughter has informed me of your dishonorable plan to sell her to this notorious lecher in payment of your debts. Such conduct must disgust any person of sensibility. When I hired Matilda as my cook—"

Mountavon had taken enough from this mealymouthed fool. "I demand my daughter at once! She is no longer to act

163

as your servant, and I have no stomach for your pious platitudes!''

"She is of age, and I need a cook," the stubborn fellow insisted.

Mountavon played his ace. "If she's not here in five minutes, I'll lay a complaint of abduction with the nearest magistrate and smear your name and hers throughout Scotland!''

"Try that and I'll kill you," said the soldier gently.

Even Tark, prepared to enjoy the humiliation of the bungling idiot who had given him so much trouble for no profit, was appalled at this last remark. He opened his mouth to voice a protest but was effectively silenced when the terrible laird said icily, "One word—one *syllable*—from you, Tark, and it's the moat. I mean that!''

One look at his face convinced the earl that he did.

But it was Mountavon who had the last word.

"My debts!" he stuttered. "S-s-surely my own daughter would not s-s-see her parents thrown into the s-s-streets to s-s-starve?''

Matilda, who had been sharply commanded by her laird to remain in the Great Hall with their guests, had naturally lost no time in following him. She made her excuses to Lady Margaret and hurried after her husband. The older woman, hoping to get the details from her young protégée later, willingly agreed to assume the role of hostess. Matilda lost no time in finding out from Fredricks where the antagonists had gone. She must be near the major, to give help if needed! She had listened just outside the open door and had been, as usual, both impressed and delighted by her dear husband's force of character. How firmly, how easily, how adroitly, he had handled a situation that had so terrified her!

But there was something about her father's final wail that touched her heart. How could those two foolish people survive such a disaster? While she was wringing her hands nervously, wondering if she could bear to ask her splendid husband to help such uncaring people, the matter was solved for her in a strange way. The major changed from icy anger to good humor with a speed that would have made McLeod suspicious.

"I understand you are a betting man, Mountavon," he said in a voice whose smooth, worldly suavity startled Matilda as much as it did his uninvited guests.

Tark snorted, but Mountavon, ever reckless, ever hopeful, and quite ignoring the heavy irony in the major's voice, said eagerly, "I will bet upon anything!"

The fellow's actually proud of it! mused the major. Well, it will make my task easier.

"I offer you a wager, milord," he said easily. "If your daughter comes into this room in the next two minutes and the Earl of Tark announces that he will *not* marry her, he will cancel thereby all your gambling debts, and if not I shall pay them."

Confused but so eager to accept this amazing wager that he was fairly stuttering, Matilda's father agreed to the conditions. Tark knew a deep thrust of uneasiness—how could the huge bumpkin be so sure of a patent impossibility? Perhaps he was not aware of the amount of the debt or of Tark's urgent, *crucial* need to produce an heir to placate the obdurate, bitter trustees of his estates.

The great fellow was staring down at them from his hulking height, a smile tugging at his lips. How *dare* he laugh at Tark? With a sense of shock, the earl noted the empty sleeve of the dress jacket folded neatly. How dare a crippled ex-soldier challenge his betters? Tark leaned forward. "It's a sure thing, Mountavon! You know I must marry now. Take the wager!"

"Done!" gasped Mountavon, looking at the laird.

"Done," said the laird with his stupid smile. "Shall we drink a glass of brandy while we wait—to celebrate the wager?"

"Oh, no, you don't!" Tark halted McLeod's movement toward the door. "We'll have no servants running off to set up a rig! Two minutes, you said?" He made an elaborate play of consulting his big gold pocket watch. "I'm afraid it's down to one minute now, sir—or less!"

Matilda knew her duty. She swept into the muniment room, head held very high, wide golden eyes blazing, looking every inch a loved and loving bride in her white gown. She met her husband's smile with one of her own.

"You wanted me, Laird Bruce?" She pouted her lips at him in the gesture she knew he loved.

The major gave his full-throated laugh. "I *knew* you'd disobey me and eavesdrop outside the door, my little battle-maid!" Moving around the desk to take her hand, he grinned at the stunned men facing him. "Gentlemen, make your bow to my wife." He smiled. "It appears you will not be able to marry her yourself, Tark. Your loss!"

The loaded words infuriated the dissolute earl so greatly that his hands clenched into claws, but he did not attack. There was something imposing about that huge, controlled body that warned that, crippled or not, he would not be an easy man to destroy. The earl was a seasoned gamester. He shrugged and forced a smile.

"Tricky, but you have won. I can hardly offer for a married woman." He cast a scornful glance at the white-faced Mountavon. "Better beg your new son-in-law to put you up for the night. Or sell you a horse to get you to London. I'm leaving at once, and I'm afraid there will not be room in my carriage for you."

Without a further word or glance, he strode from the room. The major nodded at McLeod, who went silently after, to see the fellow off the premises. The major stood regarding his unwelcome kinsman-by-law.

"I suppose I shall have to put you up for the night," he said at length. "When McLeod returns, I'll have him conduct you to a room and bring supper to you there. I'm sure you are too *tired* to attend our celebration tonight. Our new neighbors are just beginning to accept us." He fell into his newly learned Scots burr. "Ah canna' jeopardize ma mixty-maxty standin' in the community wi' such a tale as ye might babble." Then he dropped dialect; he was not smiling. "When he discovered we were married, Tark would never have forgiven your debts. He would have ruined you. My wager saved you. Will he honor his word?"

Mountavon nodded. A little color was returning to his cheeks. He could hardly comprehend his good fortune or accept that the stolid soldier had so neatly outwitted the wily earl, but already his brain was busy with schemes to exploit his new son-in-law.

"I shall send for Lady Mountavon," he began pompously. "She will wish to make the acquaintance of her daughter's husband."

"You will return to London tomorrow," corrected the soldier firmly. "I shall give you a comfortable carriage and supply two grooms to get you safely there. Together with the saving of your fortune and your house, I believe that is sufficient." His gaze was hard. "It is customary for the gifts to be given to the bride, not her parents. However, I shall accept your absence—your continued absence—as a suitable wedding gift. I bid you good night. Please remain here until Sergeant McLeod comes to conduct you to your room."

Shrugging, Mountavon watched as the soldier led Matilda out of the room. Who would have guessed that the plain little wench could catch herself such a prize? When the soldier cooled down, a clever man might get more out of him. Well, he had his money and his house back, and he'd steer clear of the earl in future, but he wouldn't talk about the wager in London. The memory of Tark's bitter, defeated expression returned.

"The soldier fleeced us neatly," he murmured. "And I'll wager Tark won't be talking about it either!" He settled into a chair, waiting for the good meal and comfortable bed he had been promised.

Leading his darling wife back into the Great Hall, the major felt deeply satisfied. And amused. Matilda'd been a good partner, *risen* to it, the little fighter, just as he had hoped she would when he gave her that abrupt command to stay in place as he left the Hall with the two rascals. Now all he had to do was carry off the rest of the evening, with her help and that of the loyal servants. And the friends he and Matilda had made, the major added, with a warm feeling under his breastbone. Most of these people, while they were justifiably curious, were too well-bred to show their curiosity.

Cullan made a strong diversion. Whether it was because of the quality and amount of his host's whisky he had imbibed or because of feelings of goodwill normally uncharacteristic of him, the noted recluse showed himself to be a splendid guest, telling rousing tales of the ancient glories of Glenholme and relating quite-scandalous anecdotes about the "auld laird." When he had all the men laughing over his ribald stories and even the ladies tittering helplessly, he summoned Conal to bring in his "wee giftie to the laird."

To everyone's amazement, it was a fine set of bagpipes.

The major accepted them with real pleasure. "I have always wanted to learn to play a set o' the pipes," he confessed, to general amusement. "I don't suppose right now is a good time to learn?"

Upon being raucously assured that it would be a very *bad* time for everyone within earshot of the squawking he'd inevitably make, he surrendered the pipes to Conal, with instructions to deliver them to McLeod for safekeeping.

Conal took them with a slight grin, and then, in the cheerful spirit of the evening, dared greatly.

"Sir, d'ye mean ye willna' ask my laird to play for ye?"

Lord Cullan tried to look angry, but even behind the beard, it was plain to see he desired to show off his skills. He was soon persuaded, and after the appropriate preparations, he began to stride up and down in a space hastily cleared for him.

"Ma *first* tune," he began, amid apprehensive laughter, "is a salute to the new laird. I call it 'Hail to the Chief'!" And he proceeded to play that, and later some lightsome reels for dancing.

It was the best night Castle Glenholme had seen in a hundred years. At least, so said the guests, when, weary but pleased, they began to wend their way home after a tasty breakfast.

Matilda, whose patience had grown thinner as the night advanced, could hardly wait to see the last of the guests out the door before turning to her exasperating husband with the demand, "*Now tell me!* What do you intend to do next?"

It was a rhetorical question, but the major took full advantage of it. Eyes glinting wickedly, he took his little bride under his arm. Then, in the manner of a schoolmaster instructing a slow pupil, he began pedantically, "First, I shall escort you to our chamber—our marital chamber. Safely closeted there, I intend to teach you a great many ways to please me, since I am sure you will agree that I deserve a fulsome reward for my efforts on your behalf this night. Then, my beloved wife, my darling, my own Merielle, I shall—" He bent to kiss those soft lips.

Merielle! Matilda uttered so huge a sigh of joy that her bold soldier felt repaid for anything he had done. She was putting up her arms adoringly to pull his face down to hers for another kiss. Ignoring any observers, the major eagerly assisted her endeavors. She kissed him with deep passion—a woman's kiss.

She felt a tremor go through the big body pressed against hers.

"You are learning fast," muttered the soldier. "I think we had better hasten upstairs. My knees are suddenly feeling weak."

"Have no fear," his little battle-maid said lovingly. "I shall take care of you, husband—always!"

Close-linked, they turned to mount the wide stone stairway to their rooms. The major was the first to become aware of the long line of tired but admiring faces.

Every servant in the castle had come to pay tribute to the acknowledged laird. Fredricks was there, beside Miss Alford; Ian and Colin Wallace, McLeod, Polly, Jem, all the maids and grooms, all smiling!

Weary as he was, and hungry to share the comfort of his bed with his little wife, the major could not resist that row of loyal and proud servants. He stood tall and gave them his best salute. And then he went down the line, calling every one by name. When he returned to Matilda again, he said to them,

"My thanks to all of you. I could not have won my battle without you. I hope and pray we shall all have a long and happy life at Glenholme, our castle now by right of your courage and loyal devotion. My wife and I thank you, and bid you good night!"

Then the laird and Matilda went up the stairs to the accompaniment of cheers and shouts of "Bruce! Bruce!"

Matilda was crying, too moved to speak.

When he had their door shut and his love close against him, the major whispered whimsically, "See what you've gotten me into, with your promise that I should win my battle? Ian tells me he's a dab on the pipes and wishes to become the official piper for the laird. Colin demands to be my page and live in the castle. *Everyone* wants to serve the laird and magnify my consequence!" He groaned theatrically. "I shall never be able to be plain Major Bruce again!" Gently he kissed the tears from her cheeks.

Merielle's dazzling smile broke through the tears.

"But you never *were* plain Major Bruce, my darling," she whispered. "You have always been—the laird."